"We aren't so different, you and I,"

Cruz said quietly.

He was right, Josie thought. In more ways than she could have imagined. The realization was a shock.

So was what happened next.

Lost in thought, she hadn't noticed him moving closer until she felt his palm against her cheek. Startled, she turned and stared straight into his face.

"Why so sad?" he asked in a husky whisper.

"I—I don't know," she replied. "It just seems life isn't fair, and it's the young and innocent who suffer most."

"You suffered, didn't you, Josie?" He brushed his thumb over her brow. "You still do."

"No." She tried to turn away, but his soft touch immobilized her. "I—I'm happy with my life," she stammered. "I have everything I want, everything I need."

"Everything?" he asked softly.

Dear Reader,

In September, we've got an extra special surprise for you! There's been so much enthusiasm for our DIAMOND JUBILEE titles, that this month we've got two DIAMOND JUBILEE books for you by two of your favorite authors: Annette Broadrick with *Married?!* and Dixie Browning with *The Homing Instinct*.

The DIAMOND JUBILEE—Silhouette Romance's tenth anniversary celebration—is our way of saying thanks to you, our readers. To symbolize the timelessness of love, as well as the modern gift of the tenth anniversary, we're presenting readers with a DIAMOND JUBILEE Silhouette Romance each month, penned by one of your favorite Silhouette Romance authors. In the coming months, writers such as Stella Bagwell, Lucy Gordon and Phyllis Halldorson are writing DIAMOND JUBILEE titles especially for you.

And that's not all! There are six books a month from Silhouette Romance—stories by wonderful writers who time and time again bring home the magic of love. During our anniversary year, each book is special and written with romance in mind. September brings you *Romeo in the Rain* by Kasey Michaels—a sequel to her heart-warming *His Chariot Awaits*. And in the coming months works by such loved writers as Diana Palmer, Brittany Young and Victoria Glenn are sure to put a smile on your lips.

During our tenth anniversary, the spirit of celebration is with us year-round. And that's all due to you, our readers. With the support you've given us, you can look forward to many more years of heartwarming, poignant love stories.

I hope you'll enjoy this book and all of the stories to come. Come home to romance—Silhouette Romance—for always!

Sincerely,

Tara Hughes Gavin
Senior Editor

DIANA WHITNEY

Scout's Honor

Silhouette Romance
Published by Silhouette Books New York
America's Publisher of Contemporary Romance

To Joan Tomchak,
with gratitude for your
friendship and support

SILHOUETTE BOOKS
300 E. 42nd St., New York, N.Y. 10017

ISBN: 0-373-08745-4

First Silhouette Books printing September 1990

Printed in the U.S.A.

Books by Diana Whitney

Silhouette Romance

O'Brian's Daughter #673
A Liberated Man #703
Scout's Honor #745

Silhouette Special Edition

Cast a Tall Shadow #508
Yesterday's Child #559

DIANA WHITNEY

says she loves "fat babies and warm puppies, mountain streams and Southern California sunshine, camping, hiking and gold prospecting. Not to mention strong, romantic heroes!" She married her own real-life hero fifteen years ago. With his encouragement, she left her longtime career as a municipal finance director and pursued the dream that had haunted her since childhood—writing. To Diana, writing is a joy, the ultimate satisfaction. Reading, too, is her passion, from spine-chilling thrillers to sweeping sagas, but nothing can compare to the magic and wonder of romance.

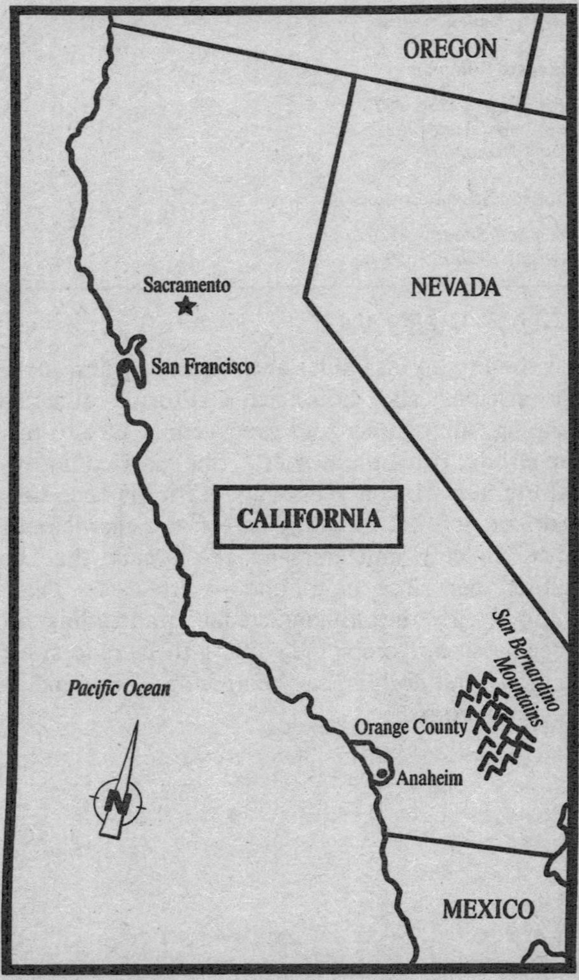
OREGON
NEVADA
Sacramento
San Francisco
CALIFORNIA
San Bernardino Mountains
Pacific Ocean
Orange County
Anaheim
N
MEXICO

Chapter One

Where in the hell was this McGee woman, anyway?

Cruz Erickson checked his watch for the umpteenth time and paced another lap on the small wood-planked porch. Irritation was developing into serious annoyance.

On Southern California's fast track, impatience was a common malady and for Cruz the ailment was chronic. Today he'd postponed an important production meeting for this fruitless fiasco and a dull headache did little to improve his sour mood.

Such tardiness was inexcusable, he fumed silently, particularly for one holding herself as a role model for impressionable youngsters.

Cruz had finally decided that he'd cooled his heels long enough when a bellowing motorcyle screeched to a stop in front of the tiny frame house. He glared at the noisy intruder.

The helmeted driver, leather-clad and booted like a storm trooper, revved the huge bike with deft wrist flicks. Cruz winced at the ear-splitting din. The biker flipped off the ignition, dismounted with a surprisingly fluid movement and stared at the porch through a gray-tinted visor before marching resolutely toward Cruz.

A jealous boyfriend, Cruz thought, absently rubbing his throbbing temple. This is just perfect.

With a smart pivot, Cruz spun and strode down the peeling wooden steps. "You're out of luck," he said crisply, stepping around the helmeted person. "She's not home."

The headpiece tilted quizzically. "Mr. Erickson?"

Cruz lurched to a stop. The voice was soft, melodic and undeniably feminine. Could it possibly...? Oh, no.

Slowly, Cruz peered back over his shoulder and saw a mound of short coppery curls framing a curious snub-nosed face. The apple-red helmet was now tucked under her arm, exposing an odd dangle of feather-and-bead earrings swishing below her chin. The young woman flashed a dazzling smile, pulled off her leather gloves and dropped them into the helmet before extending her hand.

"You must be Billy Erickson's father," she said cheerfully, grabbing his limp hand for a vigorous shake. "I'm Josie McGee."

Cruz closed his eyes and took a deep breath. This was worse than he'd expected. His son's Boy Scout leader was some kind of Hell's Angel. No wonder Billy had been behaving so strangely.

If Josie noticed Cruz's discomfort, she made no mention of it. Instead she wrapped surprisingly firm fingers around Cruz's elbow and propelled him back toward the porch. He was too startled to offer resistance. When they reached the front door, she released her grip.

"I've been running late all day," Josie said breathlessly. "There was a mixup at the recreation facility where I work. Tiny-tot ballet class was double-scheduled with the junior basketball playoffs. You can imagine the chaos."

Her soft laugh was husky and mellow, a curious contrast to the metal-studded, black leather jacket she was unzipping. But then, her fragile face was framed by a thick mop of Shirley Temple curls that didn't exactly fit the biker mold, either.

Cruz had expected . . . Well, he hadn't really known what to expect, but reality had exceeded his wildest imagination. Billy had said that Josie McGee was different. For once Cruz had to admit that his son had not exaggerated.

Josie shrugged out of the jacket, shifting the red helmet from one arm to the other. She wore a cotton tank top too loose to be immodest, but revealing enough to capture Cruz's attention. Beneath that shroud of heavy leather was a very slender and shapely young woman.

Cruz was vaguely aware that Josie had been chatting nonstop, but he'd been too distracted to concentrate on what she'd been saying. He cleared his throat. "Pardon me?"

Draping her jacket over the helmet, Josie squinted up. "Have you been waiting long?" Cruz opened his mouth to answer but Josie was already on the next subject. "I was really pleased when you called to request a meeting. You're the only parent who has shown any interest at all in the troop. They don't mean to be ambivalent, of course—"

Josie stopped talking long enough to dig a key from her jeans pocket with her free hand and open the front door; then she snagged Cruz's elbow again and towed him inside, chatting cheerfully. "It's just a matter of having enough time, I suppose. Would you like some coffee?"

"No, thank y—"

"Neither would I. Too hot." She tossed the leather-wrapped helmet on a lumpy sofa, which was covered with a worn bedspread, then strode into the tiny kitchen and opened the fridge. "Soda or iced tea?"

Cruz followed her. "Neither. Ms. McGee, I haven't much time—" A loud squawk startled him. He spun around and saw a huge green parrot on a T-shaped perch, glaring malevolently.

The bird cocked its head, screeched again, then said, "Outta' here, jerk."

"Quiet, Walter," Josie mumbled, still peering into the refrigerator.

Walter flapped his stubby wings. "Throw the bum out. awwrk . . . kill the umpire."

Cruz stared at the creature. "A charming pet."

"Ummm? Oh, his previous owner was a real sports nut. Walter picked up some of the man's more colorful expressions." Josie glanced over her shoulder and spoke to the bird. "*Invictus*, Walter."

The green head twisted grotesquely and Walter blinked tiny yellow eyes. "'Master of fate'," the bird squawked hoarsely. "'Captain of soul' . . . ark . . . Henley, Henley." Walter finished the recitation with a flutter and a piercing shriek.

Josie flashed another devastating smile. "I've been trying to put a little class into his act. Walter still prefers colorful idioms to poetry, but eventually he'll come around."

Cruz felt as though he'd eaten Alice's mushrooms and had come face-to-face with one of the Mad Hatter's crazy cronies. He wanted nothing more at this point than to simply take care of business and get the hell out of this wacky Wonderland.

Frustrated, he squared his shoulders and briskly extended his hand in a no-nonsense, take-charge gesture. "Ms. McGee, I—"

Josie slapped a cold can into his palm. "I hope diet cola is okay."

"Uh . . . yes, it's fine, thank you." Cruz stared numbly at the dripping can, listened to the squawking parrot and realized that he'd completely lost control of this ridiculous situation.

A scraping sound grabbed his attention and he saw Josie had pulled two chrome-and-vinyl chairs away from a wobbly but scrupulously clean table. Josie sat, gesturing for Cruz to join her, then popped the tab on her drink and took a healthy swallow.

As the fizzy liquid flowed down her parched throat, Josie gathered her thoughts and eyed her bewildered visitor. So this was Billy Erickson's widowed father, the man whose unreasonably high expectations had turned his poor son into an eleven-year-old senior citizen. Josie had pictured someone older, distinguished and slick, with a haughty gaze and a superior manner. Instead she saw a man in his very early thirties with tousled blond hair and puppy-brown eyes, looking completely baffled and endearingly awkward.

Of course, looks could certainly be deceiving. Josie knew that only too well. But from the shoulders of his smartly tailored suit and silk power tie to the soles of his expensive imported shoes, the man definitely dressed the part of an up-and-coming executive. It's just that his face didn't fit the rest of the image. Cruz Erickson carried himself proudly, with great authority, yet there was a glimmer of uncertainty in those dark eyes that revealed a core of softness, perhaps even compassion.

Josie watched Cruz glance around her small home and saw something else in his expression—overt disapproval. She felt a small twinge. After thumbing her nose at convention for years, reproachful looks had never bothered her—until now.

Shifting uncomfortably, Cruz swept the area with a practiced eye. The kitchen, dining and living rooms were all visible, and he noted a colorful motocross poster, professionally framed in sparkling glass, hanging in the tiny living room. A loose basketball lay on the floor beside an armchair piled with child-sized baseball mitts.

The furnishings were obviously old and well used, but in spite of the clutter Cruz noted that the floors were sparkling clean and the kitchen counter gleamed as though waxed.

Finally Cruz stiffly seated himself and placed the unopened soda can on the table. It was time to get this over with. He cleared his throat. "I must admit to being somewhat surprised that a young single woman like yourself would take on the responsibilities of a Boy Scout troop."

Huge hazel eyes scanned Cruz playfully. Josie seemed to be enjoying his discomfort and she paused to take another swallow of soda before replying. "Why is that so surprising to you?"

"I suppose I was expecting someone, well..." Cruz tugged at his suddenly tight collar, crooking his necktie as he struggled to choose just the right words. "Ah, someone older with more experience and—"

"And an XY chromosome?" Smiling sweetly, Josie reached out and straightened Cruz's tie. The intimate gesture startled him as much as the impudent question. Josie simply leaned back, obviously amused. "Lighten up, Mr. Erickson. I may not sweat testosterone but I can stoke a drill-and-bow fire as well as any man."

Cruz squirmed. "Your gender is not a problem."

"What a relief," Josie replied with exaggerated drama and a devilish glint in her eye. "Then what, exactly, *is* the problem?"

"Well, one would expect a troop leader to have some actual Scout experience." Cruz winced, realizing that his reply sounded more like a weak question than a hard-nosed statement of fact.

Josie pursed her lips thoughtfully. "I was a Girl Scout. Will that do?"

"That's hardly the same," Cruz responded, his tone colored by the merest hint of disdain.

Josie hitched one eyebrow, but said nothing. She didn't have to. Cruz knew perfectly well that he sounded like a hard-core chauvinist and his own verbal clumsiness irritated him immensely.

Good Lord, what was wrong with him? This petite woman had deftly turned the tables, putting him on the defensive. Cruz hadn't a clue as to how she'd accomplished that clever feat, but he wasn't accustomed to losing control.

Annoyance edged his voice, making it harsher than he'd intended. "Actually, Ms. McGee, I couldn't care less whether you're female or not. My problem is with the attitude you're instilling in the boys."

The amused twinkle faded from Josie's eyes. She looked startled and, to Cruz's surprise, a bit hurt. He suppressed the unexpected guilty prickle, reminding himself that his primary responsibility was to his son. To be complacent about the kind of guidance Billy received from adult role models would be tantamount to child neglect.

Fortified by the thought, Cruz met Josie's confused expression with determination. "How many boys are in the troop?"

Josie regarded him thoughtfully, then answered, "Eight."

"And how many have increased rank since you took over?"

"One, but—"

"Don't you think that's a rather poor statistic?"

"I believe in encouraging, not forcing."

"That's admirable, but not terribly realistic." Cruz noted her eyes flash, but she said nothing. He leaned forward. "Why are you involved in a Boy Scout troop in the first place?"

Josie took a deep breath, her eyes never wavering from Cruz's stern face. She was angry. This man was pompous and arrogant and a total pain in the posterior, but she couldn't afford the luxury of telling him so. Alienating parents would be a disservice to the boys, and the troop's well-being was Josie's major concern.

Swallowing her annoyance, she managed a calm tone. "I'm involved because nobody else wanted to do it."

Cruz's gaze flickered away. Josie saw misery in his eyes and knew her words had nicked a sensitive area. Deriving no pleasure from his obvious chagrin, Josie softened her voice. "As you probably know, Joe Donaldson organized the troop about six months ago. Joe and I both worked for the city recreation department, so when he moved back east and couldn't get any of the boys' parents to take over, I volunteered. I already knew most of the kids from the playground and I just didn't want to see the troop fold. Kids deserve a few hours a week to blow off steam and have fun."

Cruz frowned. "I thought the purpose of the Boy Scouts was to instill discipline and train the boys for adult responsibilities."

Pursing her lips, Josie absently twirled the damp soda can. "This is not a paramilitary organization. Scouting offers opportunities to teach teamwork, develop friendships and nourish a love of God and country. In my opinion, however, the main purpose is simply to allow children to have fun. They'll have a lifetime of those 'adult responsibilities'. Childhood is much too brief to be wasted."

"I don't consider teaching youngsters basic social values to be a waste," Cruz replied coolly. "The world is full of puerile adults, unable to cope with reality and smothered by the burden of their own immaturity."

Crossing his arms, Cruz leaned back and challenged Josie with a look that dared her to dispute him.

She chose a different strategy. "You're right," she agreed casually, pleased by his surprised expression. "It takes all kinds—that's what makes life so interesting. Pesonally I believe the irresponsible people to whom you are referring were more likely molded by parental apathy than a lack of discipline. Still, you have a right to your opinion." Before Cruz could recover Josie tossed another curve. "You must admit that Billy has changed a lot in the past few months."

Cruz's expression hardened and his jaw twitched tensely. "As a matter of fact, that's what I wanted to speak with you about. Billy *has* changed, but not necessarily for the better."

"You're joking." Josie couldn't quite believe what she was hearing. "Two months ago Billy was so shy he'd turn pink if anyone even looked at him. The other kids teased him mercilessly, and at my first two meetings, I never even heard the sound of his voice." Standing quickly, Josie knotted her hands behind her back and paced the small kitchen. "Now Billy has made friends, his eyes sparkle, and last week he actually told a joke to the entire troop. How can you say that kind of change isn't for the better?"

"His grades are dropping," Cruz snapped. "Last week he told his grandmother to 'lighten up' and not to 'sweat the small stuff.'"

Josie winced, recognizing the philosophy as her own. "I've never condoned disrespect. I'll speak to him at the next meeting."

"I've already spoken to my son and I'm not certain that Billy will be attending the next meeting."

Josie's head snapped around. "Surely you're not thinking of taking him out of the troop."

"Actually, Ms. McGee, that's precisely what I'm considering."

Cruz watched Josie carefully. Her distress was genuine and he felt a stab of regret. In spite of her rebellious appearance, the woman seemed articulate and educated, and exuded genuine warmth when she spoke of the boys. Still, Cruz took his parental duties seriously. He felt deeply that it was never too soon for a boy to become a man, to build self-discipline and strong moral fiber.

Cruz had seen the tragedy of the wild, thrill-seeking lifestyle this woman appeared to advocate. He was familiar with the type and he was sadly familiar with the disastrous results.

Death was an unforgiving master, accepting no apology, offering no second chance; it tore the heart out of innocence and destroyed hope for the future. Death was forever.

Cruz knew this from bitter experience. And no matter what the cost he would not allow Billy to self-destruct. Cruz had already lost a brother; he'd not lose his beloved son.

Josie cradled the receiver and tried to swallow her panic. Resting her head on her desk, she ignored the thuds and childish squeals outside her office and concentrated on how to handle this unfortunate turn of events.

The office door flew open.

Sally, Josie's assistant, bounced into the room and perched on a nearby chair. "We had a bingo crisis," Sally announced. "Six balls are missing. Old Mrs. Fabbish beat the machine with her cane and threatened to sue us all for fraud."

Moaning, Josie stood. She didn't need this.

Sally grinned smugly and motioned Josie to sit. "I handled it."

Josie raised one eyebrow. "Oh? How did you manage that?"

"I gave her five free cards and hid her cane."

Smothering a smile, Josie complimented Sally on her resourcefulness, then saw a spiky-haired boy peer through the open doorway.

Josie spoke to the youngster. "What do you need, Justin?"

The boy's eyes shifted nervously. "Uh, Duncan missed the backboard and the basketball went into the street." He held out a limp hunk of flattened rubber.

Shaking her head, Josie quickly filled out a requisition form, handed it to the relieved youngster and sent him scurrying to the equipment room for a replacement.

"Typical day at your friendly neighborhood rec center," Sally mused.

Josie uttered a neutral sound and gazed out the office window.

"What's wrong, Josie? You look like you've lost your best friend—which of course you haven't, because *I'm* your best friend."

"I've got a problem." Sighing, Josie speared her fingers through her thick sorrel curls. "I just got a call from Wadsworth P. Wellington, who just happens to be the chair of Troop 161's charter committee."

Sally wrinkled her nose. "I know him. He's a stodgy old devil. Tried to break up senior-citizen bingo by declaring it a violation of the state gambling laws."

"Technically it is," Josie pointed out. "But certain charitable and religious organizations have been exempted. Perhaps he doesn't feel that the seniors' group qualified under the legal definitions."

"Sometimes you just have to bend the rules a bit."

"Well, Mr. Wellington doesn't hold with bending rules and neither does Cruz Erickson." Josie stared morosely at her friend. "He's been asking questions about me."

"Wellington?"

"No, Erickson. You know, Billy's father."

"Ah." Sally frowned. "What kind of questions?"

"The kind that subtly indicate that I may not be a proper role model for impressionable Boy Scouts. He asked Mr. Wellington about my qualifications." Josie rubbed her forehead in frustration. "I should have seen this coming. He was so darn self-righteous last night, so judgmental—"

"Last night?" Sally leaned forward, her interest piqued.

"Yes. He's not pleased by the troop's direction—thinks the boys should be spit-and-polish trained like miniature marines." Anger bubbled into Josie's voice, sharpening her words. "Of course, he hasn't volunteered to actually *do* anything—he just wants to tell *me* how to do things."

Sally was quiet for a moment, then said, "You're really hurt by this, aren't you?"

"Hurt?" Josie considered this and was surprised to realize that that was exactly what she was feeling. "I guess I am a bit hurt. I thought everything was going so well. When I first met Billy, my heart went out to him. He was such a sober little boy, with those huge spectacles and wise eyes much too old for an eleven-year-old. The other kids tormented him constantly. Now he laughs and plays during meetings just like the child he has every right to be."

"So what's Mr. Erickson's complaint?"

Josie looked away and fidgeted with a paper clip. "I guess Billy's grades have dropped a bit. And he's gotten a bit, uh, smart-mouthed."

"Ummm. Are you responsible for that?"

Josie shrugged, concentrating on twisting the clip into a mass of knotted wire. "I may have inadvertently contributed to the problem. But Billy was feeling so pressured by his father's high expectations, I just wanted to see the child in him emerge."

Standing, Sally walked slowly to the door, then turned and spoke seriously. "You're one of the most intelligent, down-to-earth people I've ever met. You'll do what's best for Billy because you know what the poor kid is going through. You've been there." Then Sally turned and walked out of the office.

Josie closed her eyes. Yes, she *had* been there. Like so many of the children she worked with, Josie's early years had been filled with hardship, burdened by adult responsibilities. She, too, had been the product of a lost childhood.

As a small girl, Josie could remember looking in the mirror at her own pinched face and huge wise eyes. She was still haunted by memories of one particular night. It hadn't started much differently than other such nights, except the air had seemed colder and the blackness more foreboding.

It had been the first night that Josie's mother had not come home; but it hadn't been the last.

Josie remembered pacing the small living room of their mobile home, waiting and worrying, suppressing tears and vivid mind pictures of imagined horrors.

What if Lena never came home? little Josie had wondered. It could happen. Abandonment had already touched Josie's young life. Lena had been a frightened pregnant teenager when Josie's father had disappeared. Could this be the night when her mother, too, left forever? Then Josie would be completely alone. The very thought had left her stiff with terror.

Then Josie recalled hearing the familiar scratch of a key searching the lock. Relief had flooded her small body as Josie wiped the wet remnants of fear from her cheeks. Opening the door, she'd seen Lena swaying drunkenly. Her mother's condition was sadly familiar, as was the pathetic role reversal between mother and child, perfected over long agonizing years. Lena had giggled like a guilty child; Josie had scolded like an indignant parent.

Little Josie had been strong and brave and oh-so-dependable as she'd tucked her tipsy mother in bed.

But alone, in the quiet of her own tiny room, little Josie McGee had pulled the covers over her head and cried herself to sleep.

In the exclusive Anaheim Hills, Cruz drove up to his parents' Tudor-style home. Eyes stinging from twelve solid hours of paperwork, he glanced at the rising moon. It was late, past Billy's bedtime. Again.

Quickly Cruz strode up the cobblestone walk. When the massive front door opened, Isabel Erickson greeted her son with a warm hug.

"Cook prepared an excellent pot roast this evening, *mi hijo*. Shall I warm it for you?" As was Isabel's habit, she still lapsed into familial Spanish for "my son." Although Isabel had been in the United States for almost forty years, she'd often said that her native tongue conveyed a greater depth of feeling in terms of endearment than did her adopted language.

Wearily Cruz refused his mother's offer. "I've eaten, thanks. But I wouldn't refuse a cup of your wonderful coffee."

Isabel laughed softly and Cruz felt the tension seep from his shoulders. In contrast to her husband's serious manner, Isabel Erickson laughed frequently. To Cruz, the mellow sound was a soothing reminder of his early childhood. He used to lie awake at night, listening to his mother's lilting voice and gentle laughter. Then, knowing that all must be right with the world, he would drift into a contented sleep.

But that had been before the accident that had destroyed Cruz's childhood and altered the course of his life.

"Cruz?" Isabel touched a soft red-tipped finger to his cheek, startling him.

"Pardon me?"

"Here is your coffee."

Smiling his thanks, Cruz took the china cup and sipped the rich European brew. As always it was wonderful. Isabel roasted and ground the coffee beans herself, guarding the secret she'd carried from her native Spain.

As were many north-country Spaniards, Isabel was fair-skinned and blond, with expressive brown eyes that had passed to succeeding generations. In college, she had fallen in love with Gunther T. Erickson, a burly man of Scandinavian descent. With their marriage, America became Isabel's new home, and although she loved her adopted country, Cruz knew that his mother dreamed of returning to visit her homeland. Someday Cruz hoped to make that dream come true.

"Dad, look!" Billy burst into the expansive parlor, arms laden with wads of colorful fabric. "Look what Grandmama bought for me."

Cruz set the cup on the smoked-glass table and squatted to inspect his son's treasures. "Well, what have we got here?"

Dropping to his knees, Billy carefully spread the items over the plush carpet and poked his slipping eyeglasses back into place. Billy held up a blue sack with straps and zippers everywhere. "It's a knapsack. I can use it on the camp-out next weekend. Josie says it's gonna be so fun—we get to sleep in tents and everything."

Camp out? Cruz felt a hot knot in his stomach.

Before Cruz could respond, Billy hoisted a lump of rumpled orange fabric. "It's a brand-new pup tent. Look, it even has the Scout logo on it. Isn't it neat?"

Cruz nodded sickly. There was no easy way to tell Billy that there may not be a camp-out. In fact, given Mr. Wellington's reaction to their telephone conversation, Cruz was well aware that by next week, Troop 161 might not even exist.

That thought disturbed Cruz. All he'd wanted was to prudently research Josie McGee's background, but Wellington had completely overreacted. Belatedly Cruz had remembered that Wellington's firm was dependent on loans from Gunther Erickson's bank. In retrospect Cruz realized that Wellington would probably have fired his own mother to please Gunther.

Wellington was a cowardly old fogy, Cruz thought in disgust, wishing he'd never made that damn phone call.

Now Cruz turned his attention to his son, who was still rattling on about pup tents and camp-outs and Josie McGee. Billy was so excited, Cruz determined that no matter what Wellington did, there *would* be a camping trip even if Cruz had to carry every one of those boys up the mountain piggyback.

One thing was for sure—Cruz would be going on that camp-out. Besides, it would provide an excellent opportunity to spend precious time with Billy.

Cruz tousled his son's hair. "These are wonderful presents. Did you thank Grandmama?"

Billy nodded vigorously. "I can't wait till next week. It's gonna be more fun than I've ever had in my whole life."

Cruz cleared his throat. "I'm sure it will, but now it's about time to go home and get some shut-eye. Go on upstairs and get the rest of your things."

"Okay." Billy scooped up his precious camping equipment and dashed out of the room.

Isabel had been watching quietly. "Billy seems to be quite enamored of his new Scout leader." Cruz shifted uncomfortably, but didn't respond. Isabel prodded gently. "What is she like?"

"She's . . . different."

Isabel nodded, folding her hands primly in her lap and leaning forward to indicate interest. "I would assume so. Handling a group of exuberant boys would take a woman of great strength and dedication. What do you know about her?"

Playing for time, Cruz reached for his cup and took a slow sip of lukewarm coffee. He didn't really want to get into a discussion of Josie McGee right now, and he didn't really know why. He found thoughts of her... disturbing. But Isabel was waiting patiently and Cruz realized that by avoiding the subject his mother's curiosity would be piqued. It would be best to retire the matter by answering her questions.

"Ms. McGee works as the supervisor for the city's recreation center." Cruz balanced the saucer on his knee, staring into the cup as though reading tea leaves. "According to the chairman of the troop's charter committee, she graduated from some university in Texas. Apparently she majored in psychology and physical education."

"Adequate qualifications, I would think."

"On paper."

Isabel arched a shapely brow. "Do I detect a note of disapproval?"

Cruz sighed. "As a role model, she leaves a bit to be desired. She rides a motorcycle."

"Gracious, how shocking." Isabel's lips twitched and Cruz felt his face heat.

"You know what I mean," he mumbled.

"No, not really."

"The woman is like a defiant teenager." Cruz was surprised by his sharp tone and made an effort to sound more casual. "Ms. McGee has this theory that free expression shouldn't be constrained by such tacky notions as duty and responsibility. I find her if-it-feels-good-do-it attitude to be self-indulgent and irresponsible."

A frown marred Isabel's forehead and her hands clasped fretfully. "That is quite distressing. I would have thought one devoting so much time to young people would be a caring and emotionally centered individual."

Cruz stood quickly, jamming his hands in his pockets as he roamed the room in agitation. He was upset. No, he was angry, actually shaking with leashed fury, and he had absolutely no idea why. Deep down, Cruz knew perfectly well how illogical it was to feel such inner turmoil over a woman he'd just met, but these emotions were too strong, too painful to ignore.

"Why do you dislike this woman?" Isabel asked quietly.

Cruz stopped pacing. "I don't dislike her. I hardly know her." The concern in his mother's eyes compelled Cruz to purge himself, to explain what he didn't even understand. "She seems so...wild. The woman thumbs her nose at convention, just another thrill seeker pushing life to a breakneck pace, regardless of who gets hurt. People like that are too busy having fun to recognize the pain of those who love them, those who will be left behind. She's just like Ray—"

The impact of his own words hit Cruz like a sledge.

Isabel paled, touching her throat with a small wimpering sound.

Suddenly, Cruz realized that his hands were trembling and his face was moist with icy perspiration. He felt like someone had reached into his belly and jerked out his innards.

Gradually his breathing slowed and his head cleared. Cruz realized that the emotions assaulting him—rage and pain and feelings of betrayal—had been misdirected. Josie McGee's only real crime was to remind Cruz of his wild rebellious brother. The understanding came as a serious shock to his system.

Six years older, Ramon Erickson had been Cruz's idol and in spite of the age difference they had been closer than most brothers. Cruz thought back, recalling the handsome young man with flashing eyes and a smile that could melt a glacier. The brothers had been as different in personality as in appearance: Cruz was quiet sunshine and white sand; Ray was like a neon city at midnight, colorful flashes in a world of darkness.

Like two halves of a larger being, the brothers had loved each other. Cruz had adored Ray, ignoring his faults and magnifying his virtures until reality had been distorted into the illusion of total perfection. Later Cruz would recognize that those traits he'd most admired, Ray's courage and independence, were nothing more than reckless impulse and self-indulgence.

Now, transported back in time, Cruz saw past images so vivid that it was like reliving the experience. He remembered Ray's birthday cake sporting seventeen flaming candles. It had been a joyful day, filled with excitement and laughter. Crumpled gift wrap and ribbons were still strewn across the floor when Ray had sneaked out to enjoy the gift he'd bought for himself—a shiny new car.

The cherry-red dragster spewed stenciled flames, and to young Cruz, it was an awesome, almost frightening machine. Cruz had secretly watched as Ray polished the gleaming chrome with loving care.

When Gunther Erickson found out about the car everything had struck the proverbial fan. There had been a horrible fight. The argument had been unnerving but not unusual. It seemed to young Cruz that his brother and father were always fighting about something. But that day Cruz hadn't wanted to listen. He'd gone to his room, slamming the door and covering his ears.

Something else happened later that night, something that Cruz still couldn't quite recall. Every time he brought this part of his childhood to mind, the memory died into blackness, as though a lead shield shrouded his brain, blocking subsequent events.

But Cruz could remember awakening in darkness, cold and sick with dread. He'd crept down the hallway, following the sound of his mother's sobbing.

The image faded and Cruz's mind shot forward. Now he remembered standing in soft grass, staring down at a concrete headstone bearing his brother's name.

"Cruz."

Isabel's voice touched his mind, slowly bringing Cruz back to the present. He felt his mother's hand on his arm and in her soft eyes he saw compassion and understanding.

"I know," Isabel whispered softly. "We all miss him."

Nodding, Cruz swallowed the lump in his throat and rubbed his eyelids to clear the annoying dampness.

Isabel forced a pleasant tone. "Do you remember the bicycle?"

Cruz smiled, appreciating his mother's attempt to lighten the somber mood. "I'll never forget it," he mused, recalling the happier time. "My first bike and my first broken arm."

Laughing, Isabel gave Cruz's cheek a motherly pat. "If you had not removed the training wheels, the experience would have been less painful. You were only four."

"True, but Ray dared me and in those days I couldn't resist a good dare."

"Yes, you were so adventurous then, even worse than your brother. Your nearly gave your poor father a heart attack. He was so worried about you." Her eyes twinkled. "I recall that you did not remove the wheels again."

Cruz chuckled. "No, not after coming home with a cast on my arm and finding the damned things had been welded on."

"You were so angry that you dragged the poor bicycle out to the curb and demanded that the trash truck take it away."

"A gesture I lived to regret. If I recall, I had to take meals in a standing position for several days."

As mother and son relived old times, their laughter bounced through the parlor.

A shadow fell over the room.

In the doorway loomed a large man, soberly watching the jovial scene. Isabel straightened instantly and Cruz felt the muscles in his neck bunch.

The laughter died.

Chapter Two

Seemingly unaware of the tension he'd created, Gunther Erickson strode into the room with the confidence of a victorious general. He was a tall man, impressive and powerfully built. Thick blond hair, once Gunther's proudest physical asset, had receded to mid-scalp and was marred by telling gray streaks. Still, the senior Erickson was striking, with the proud bearing and broad shoulders of a much younger man.

As Gunther surveyed the scene, his blue eyes cut like radar, sweeping the room with military precision.

Automatically Cruz stood to accept his father's firm handshake and offer a polite greeting.

Gunther's voice boomed with authority. "Working late again, I see. Good for you. Climbing the ladder of success takes long hours and sweat equity."

Although well aware of his father's philosophy on success, Cruz harbored doubts. "I'm not sure that reaching the top of that ladder is going to be worth the climb."

Gunther responded as if Cruz had committed heresy. "Of course it's worth it. A man's got to be top of the heap or he's just holding someone else up. What the hell's wrong with you, anyway?"

Cruz rubbed his head. "Just tired, I guess. I haven't spent two evenings with Billy in the last week and—"

As if on cue, the stairway vibrated under the impact of running feet. Billy skidded through the foyer, arms filled with his precious new possessions.

"I'm ready, Dad," Billy hollered. "Can I sleep in the back yard tonight? I can practice setting up my new tent—"

"Don't run in the house!" Gunther commanded roughly, then snagged Billy's shoulder, abruptly breaking his forward momentum. Parcels flew from the startled boy's grasp and Billy's eyes widened in shock.

"S-sorry, Grandpapa," he stammered, seeming to shrink under the older man's hard stare.

Cruz felt a sudden surge of anger. Reaching out, he firmly grasped his father's wrist, forcing Gunther to release Billy. At first astounded by Cruz's impulsive display, Gunther recovered quickly, glaring at the younger man with wintry eyes.

Cruz met his father's gaze without flinching. The standoff was thick with icy tension, but mercifully brief.

One corner of Gunther's taut mouth tilted up and his cold eyes warmed with grudging admiration. Still, the older man was quite obviously annoyed by any interference in his home-rule discipline.

As usual, it was Isabel's mellow voice that calmed her husband. "You have put in a very long day, *querido*. I know how tired you must be." Her melodic tone had the desired soothing effect. As Gunther's tautness dissipated, Isabel touched his sleeve and continued, "Billy is overly excited. He meant no disrespect."

Gunther inhaled deeply. Although his eyes still glittered he spoke softly. "Excitement is no excuse for a lack of self-control."

"Of course not," Isabel said demurely, placating him. "Billy has apologized for his carelessness."

Cruz released Gunther's wrist but maintained the visual stalemate while quietly speaking to Billy. "Thank Grand-mama for dinner, son, then take your things out to the car."

Billy meekly complied and Cruz noted the reflexive clench of Gunther's fist. The intimidating movement had no effect. As a child, Cruz had been petrified by that gesture and of the thunderous expression that had so frequently twisted his father's handsome face.

Such tactics were potent weapons to a youngster, but it had been many years since Gunther had been able to control Cruz. The son was now the father's equal, a turn of events Gunther refused to publicly acknowledge.

Ordinarily Cruz simply ignored Gunther's attempted domination, treating his father with respect and suppressing any urge to argue philosophical differences.

But manhandling Billy was another matter entirely. Cruz simply wouldn't stand for it.

"Dad, my tent's crooked." Billy sat heavily on the neatly mowed lawn and stared glumly at the lopsided orange cloth. "I have this pole left over—do you think that's the problem?"

Cruz stopped pruning his favorite azalea bush, glanced over his shoulder at the lumpy pile of neon fabric and managed to suppress a bark of laughter.

Dropping the shears, Cruz dusted his knees and stood, eyeing the pitiful mess with amusement. "I think that pole is supposed to hold up the middle. Let's see the instruction sheet."

Billy searched through the clutter, emitting a satisfied grunt when he uncovered the requested item. Cruz took the paper, scanning it quickly. "Ah. That's the ridge pole—see how it snaps together with the end ribs?"

Moaning, Billy slapped his forehead in dismay. "How'd I miss that?"

"You were in a hurry, that's all." Cruz ruffled his son's thick hair and gave him an encouraging pat. "When all else fails—"

"Read the instructions," Billy concluded, grinning.

"That's my boy. Need help"

"Nah, I can—Was that the doorbell?"

Cruz glanced toward the open French doors leading into the house. Billy was already galloping across the patio.

"It's probably the paperboy," Cruz called. "Would you give him the check on the foyer table, please?"

The boy's response was an affirmative mumble, so Cruz turned back to his prized garden. Although the small area sported a variety of plants, the profusion of multihued azaleas gave Cruz the most pleasure. When blooming, the entire yard was awash with vibrant scarlet, delicate pink and snowy white blossoms. It was an oasis, a tiny island of peace in Cruz's high-pressure world.

Cruz frowned at a bare area in the farthest corner, wondering if he'd have time to construct the reflecting pool this summer. It was a question he'd asked himself for five summers now, ever since his wife, Catherine, had died. She had suggested the pool, and at the time Cruz had thought it a poor idea. The last thing he'd needed was a puddle of stagnant water doubling as a mosquito-breeding ground. So Cruz had argued and balked and procrastinated until suddenly it had been too late.

Now he was still feeling guilty and he was still procrastinating.

Every year had ended with the symbolic project undone. Completing the tribute to Catherine's memory would force a final goodbye, and perhaps somewhere deep inside, Cruz wasn't ready for that ultimate farewell to the woman who had cared for him and borne his son.

Cruz and Catherine had been more friends than lovers, and although their marriage had been arranged to fulfill family expectations, they'd had a good life together. If their relationship lacked a certain passion and sparkle, neither had been concerned. They had shared the same hopes and dreams, and had been basically content.

At least Cruz had been. Over the years, he'd often wondered if Catherine had been as satisfied. But Cruz's doubts had come too late.

The illness had struck swiftly, taking Catherine when Billy was six. For five years, Cruz had been struggling not only to be a successful father but to be a successful son. For the people Cruz loved, only perfection was acceptable, so Cruz tried to be perfect, fulfilling his obligations as best he could.

Maybe he'd tried too hard. At quiet moments like this, Cruz felt a strange emptiness. Something inside him was slowly evolving. His priorities were shifting from a work-and-duty ethic to... what? He wasn't sure.

For years Cruz had been running in circles, chasing something vague and nameless, something he wasn't even certain he wanted to catch. But this year would be different, Cruz vowed. This year, he'd build that pool for Catherine. Then he could say goodbye.

"Dad! Look who's here!"

Turning, Cruz blinked in surprise. Billy was running across the patio, pink with excitement. In the doorway, looking grim and determined, stood Josie McGee.

"It's Josie," Billy announced unnecessarily.

Slowly removing his cotton work gloves, Cruz swept her with a leisurely glance. Instead of blue jeans and a T-shirt, Josie now wore gabardine slacks and a silky sleeveless top. The weird feathery earrings had been replaced by a dangle of hammered copper, which emphasized the cinnamon highlights in her curly hair.

Obviously she'd dressed up for the occasion and Cruz had to admit that the effect was, well, stimulating. The woman was damned attractive, no doubt about it.

Josie scanned the yard, then her gaze rested on the pile of orange fabric. Cruz saw her mouth twitch in amusement, then noticed a flash of white teeth as she nibbled her lower lip. The gesture was strangely erotic, drawing attention to the fact that her mouth was moist and pink and downright inviting.

Cruz felt a tightening below his navel and quickly dragged his gaze away from her mouth. The unexpected reaction surprised and irritated him. Obviously he'd been celibate too long.

Josie broke the heavy silence. "I hope I'm not interrupting anything."

Billy answered, gesturing to the sagging tent. "I was practicing for the camp-out."

Her eyes widened slightly and her pink lips formed an O. Cruz's attention was again riveted on her mouth and he wondered if the temperature had suddenly risen ten degrees.

"I have to put this pole in," Billy said importantly. "Do you want to help?"

"Sure." Josie smiled. "But I need to speak with your father for a few minutes first."

Cruz emerged from his trance. "We'll take care of the tent later, son. Why don't you go work on your science project for a few minutes?"

Billy frowned. "I don't want to."

Cruz's eyes narrowed. "Pardon me?"

Shifting uncomfortably, Billy poked at the rumpled tent with the toe of his sneaker. "I mean, what's the sense of having a project on reptiles if you won't let me have an exhibit? All the kids will have exhibits—except me."

Cruz took a deep breath and managed a stiff smile for Josie's benefit. "I didn't say you couldn't have exhibits. I said you couldn't have *live* exhibits."

"It's not fair," Billy said. "Just because you don't like snakes and lizards and stuff—"

This had gone far enough. "Go upstairs now. We'll discuss it later." Cruz's voice broached no argument and he got none.

Head dropping, the boy mumbled, "Yes, sir," and scooted into the house.

Josie watched the entire process with interest. As she'd already ascertained by their previous encounter, Cruz Erickson was a firm disciplinarian. In this particular instance, however, she didn't feel he'd been overly harsh. Billy had been surprisingly vocal in expressing his displeasure, and Josie wondered if her presence had anything to do with that. Apparently Cruz thought so. His annoyed expression seemed to hold Josie personally responsible for his son's behavior.

Well, rats. Josie had come to resolve problems, not create them. Besides, she had an idea. In fact, all modesty aside, Josie believed it was a stroke of genius. Still, she'd need Cruz's cooperation and judging from his sour expression she wasn't likely to get anything at this point except an invitation to leave.

Josie pasted on her brightest smile. After all, a woman with a psychology degree under her belt should certainly be able to soften Mr. Erickson's rigid edges a bit.

"This is a beautiful yard," she purred, gleaning a clue from the gardening equipment strewn about. "Did you landscape it yourself?"

The ploy worked. Cruz relaxed and his eyes warmed. "Yes. It's kind of a hobby."

She recognized pride in his voice and zeroed in. "I've always admired people with green thumbs."

Smiling, Cruz shrugged off her praise. "It's not all that difficult."

"It is for me. I can't even grow fungus and I don't have the heart to pull weeds. They struggle so valiantly for life and, besides, they're the only green things in my yard." She pointed toward a bush ladened with frilled orange-and-pink blossoms. "That's absolutely gorgeous. What is it?"

Cruz's eyes lit with enthusiasm. "It's a Tintoretto azalea, a deciduous plant not terribly common in this zone."

Josie's eyes glazed. "How fascinating. Tell me more."

Cruz was more than happy to oblige. For the next twenty minutes, Josie received a personal tour of his private oasis. Surprisingly Cruz's delight was contagious and she began to enjoy hearing the history of each tiny blossom.

The yard was more like a small forest than a suburban garden. Josie's tension melted away, soothed by the symphony of chirping birds and rustling branches. The fragrance of pine mingled sensually with various floral perfumes and she was actually disappointed when the tour ended.

"It's all lovely," Josie said softly, feeling a surge of pleasure at Cruz's grateful smile.

Josie, too, was grateful. She'd been privy to another side of Cruz Erickson, a side she found quite palatable. The man standing before her wore dirty-kneed jeans and a ripped T-shirt. A lock of blond hair fell sexily across his forehead, and Josie thought this earthy image considerably more attractive than the rigid immaculately-tailored executive with whom she'd faced off yesterday.

In fact at this moment Josie found Cruz Erickson more attractive than any man she'd ever met. His mouth was firm, with a hint of softness that made her shiver. And a woman could simply get lost in those dark exotic eyes.

Yes, the man was charismatic and exciting, but Josie cautioned herself that he was also dangerous. At least her reaction to him was dangerous, and Josie realized she'd do well to steer clear of such sensual thoughts.

Stepping away, Josie cleared her throat and firmly reminded herself that she'd not driven across town merely to ogle Billy's father. It was time to get down to business.

"I've been thinking about our discussion yesterday," she said crisply. "Although we obviously have differing points of view, some of your suggestions may be valid. I have a proposition for you."

She turned to face Cruz and saw a guarded expression that didn't quite conceal his surprise.

He eyed her cautiously. "What kind of proposition?"

"Nothing immmoral, I assure you," she replied cheerfully. "I'd like you to be my co-leader."

His stunned expression was comical. Turning away, Cruz rubbed the back of his neck, then glanced over his shoulder. "Why?"

"Because you obviously have an interest in your son's activities." Chin high, Josie stared him straight in the eye. "And because you seem to feel like you can do a better job than I."

He had the grace to look embarrassed. "Ms. McGee—"

"Call me Josie," she said.

"Very well...Josie." He ran his fingers through his hair. "I may have come on a bit strong yesterday and I apologize for that."

"Apology accepted. Now, will you accept the job?"

"Actually things have been rather hectic at work and I haven't had much free time lately. I'm not sure I'd be able to, ah, do the job justice," he finished lamely.

Cruz looked so miserable that Josie almost felt sorry for him. Almost, but not quite. She smiled sweetly. "I see."

Cruz flushed under her knowing stare. The woman had him cornered. He was uncomfortable but had to admit that he'd asked for it. If he refused the position, he'd have no choice but to back off and let her handle the boys in her own flighty way. Cruz had already decided that pulling Billy from the troop would be cruel and unfair, so his options were definitely limited.

He felt a blossoming respect for Josie McGee. The woman had called his bluff and, under the same circumstances, it's exactly what Cruz himself would have done. Besides, the idea was not without merit. Change could only be accomplished from a position of power, and whether the woman realized it or not, she was offering Cruz the perfect forum to instill some proper social values in those boys.

Lost in thought, Cruz absently rubbed his chin for a few minutes, then said, "All right."

The twinkle in Josie's eyes faded. "You'll do it?"

"Absolutely. I've been wanting to spend more time with Billy, anyway."

Josie frowned. This wasn't what she'd expected. She'd done a bit of checking on the rigid Mr. Erickson and discovered that he had always been a high-powered overachiever. She'd naturally assumed that a fast-track aerospace executive would be much too important to be bothered with something as mundane as running a Boy Scout troop.

Assisting, she amended mentally, not running. Josie nearly moaned aloud. She could almost hear the metallic sound of two iron wills clashing. This was one stroke of genius that had most definitely backfired.

"You'll need a uniform," she warned.

Cruz's mouth tightened into a thin white line. "You're joking."

"Rules are rules," she replied brightly. "Leaders are required to be properly attired, but don't worry. I think you'll look quite dashing with a snappy red beret tilted jauntily over your brow." The image was obviously distasteful to Cruz and Josie went in for the kill. "Of course, if you'd rather forget the whole thing—"

"Not at all," Cruz interrupted, speaking through clenched teeth. "I think it's an excellent compromise."

"Oh." Josie's smile flattened. "That's...fine. I guess it's settled then."

"I guess it is." A disturbing gleam lit Cruz's dark eyes.

Suppressing her dismay, Josie concentrated on the positive aspects of this peculiar liaison. Most troop business consisted of day-to-day drudgery, like planning meetings, scheduling outings and setting up fund-raisers. It was just a matter of time, she told herself calmly, until Cruz tired of the boring details and left the troop in peace. Then she would be free of Cruz Erickson's interference once and for all.

She managed what she hoped was a convincing smile. "Well, I'll see you at the meeting Wednesday night."

"I'm looking forward to it," Cruz said smoothly. His mind was churning. This could work out perfectly, he told himself. After all, Josie McGee was a charming young woman, but she was obviously a bit of a rebel. She was bound to tire of the boys as soon as troop business intruded upon her wild and foolish life-style. Then Cruz would be free to take over the troop and mold the boys into strong responsible young men.

It was just a matter of time.

The Scout meeting began as usual. A gaggle of khaki-clad boys screamed around the school gymnasium as though experiencing freedom for the first time in their lives. Josie had learned that the more energy the boys expended, the more likely they were to sit quietly during the business meeting.

As long as said business required less than thirty minutes, that is.

So with that result in mind, a rowdy game of tag was in full swing. As usual Josie was in the thick of things.

Twisting away, she dived behind the piano.

"Gotcha!" hollered a flushed blond youngster. "Josie's *it*."

"I am not, Donnie," Josie replied with mock indignation. "You missed the tag by a foot."

"Did not." Donnie skidded to a stop. "I got your arm."

Josie grimaced, a comical expression that tickled Donnie immensely. As the boy chuckled, Josie leapt out and whacked his shoulder. "Right you are," she sang. "But you're *it* now."

"That ain't fair!" Donnie yelled indignantly.

"*Isn't* fair," Josie corrected. "And you're absolutely right. Tag is like basketball. Never let your guard down or your opponent will sneak points on you."

Seven laughing youngsters scurried across the school gymnasium as though poor Donnie had a contagious disease. Josie saw four of the boys huddle in the corner, casting furtive glances. Meanwhile Donnie had given in gracefully and was futilely attempting to pass on the dubious honor of being *it* to a swivel-hipped youngster who led a merry chase.

Since the game had moved away from her, Josie relaxed slightly. She glanced at the clock and wondered when her illustrious co-leader would grace them with an appearance. Cruz had called this afternoon, saying that he'd be late. She hadn't been surprised. In fact, she'd have been surprised if he *hadn't* found some way to get out of the meeting. Billy had, as usual, hitched a ride with Donnie's parents so Josie didn't really expect Cruz to show up at all.

Not that she cared, of course. Certainly, it didn't matter one whit what Cruz Erickson did. Josie was just a bit peeved that he'd flaked out so early in the game, that was all. She'd thought him the type to have toughed through at least a few meetings before calling it quits.

From the corner of her eye, Josie noticed that Donnie was winking at the sneaky gang of four. She ignored a niggling alarm signal in her brain and looked up at the clock again. The boys could have another five minutes to expend their leashed energy, she decided. Then they should be pooped enough to sit still for half an hour.

Something poked Josie's arm.

"You're *it*," chortled Richard Foster.

Josie's jaw sagged. Donnie was standing across the room, grinning madly and the rest of the troop was practically in stitches. She protested. "Hey! I thought Donnie was *it*."

"He was," Richard explained patiently. "But I let him tag me when you weren't looking."

"Why on earth did you do that?"

"So you'd think Donnie was still *it*."

Josie was beginning to get the message. "You're all in this together, aren't you? What is this, pick-on-Josie night?"

"You're always telling us to work as a team for common goals," Donnie crowed. "Well, we did."

"And I was the goal?"

Billy shrugged shyly. "You always win."

"Well, you certainly put me in my place," Josie said, laughing. She felt tremendous pride in their accomplishment. They'd planned, organized and executed the maneuver in an outstanding example of teamwork. "Good job, boys. I'm proud of you."

The youngsters were so pleased by Josie's praise and so taken with their victory, they didn't notice the mischievous glint in her eye. Standing, she dusted her pants and nonchalantly walked toward the gloating group, gesturing toward a pile of folding chairs at the far wall of the gym. "Who wants to help set up?"

As Josie sauntered by, she touched each one of the five hands that shot up to volunteer. That done, she whirled, crouched and hollered, "Aha! Now you're all *it*."

With a blast of laughter and assorted squeals, the boys leaped forward and Josie was instantly blanketed under a squirming mass of giggling Scouts. "Uncle! I give up," she cried, feigning horror. "Have mercy!"

"Never!"

"We win."

"We're the champs."

"Yea-a-a-ah."

Laughter left Josie gasping for breath. She wound her arms protectively over her head. This did little to shield the determined tickles and tags, but the boys weren't hurting her. They were just having fun and in the process were winding down to a state of corrigible fatigue.

Suddenly, the squeals stopped and the boys stepped quickly away. Peeking from beneath her folded arms, Josie saw eight sober faces staring toward the doorway. She followed their gazes and felt her heart sink.

Cruz Erickson had arrived and he didn't look happy.

* * *

Observing the screaming chaos for several long minutes had tightened Cruz's stomach into a burning knot. This was even worse than he'd imagined.

Somewhere buried in that wild tangle of arms and legs lurked the "adult" charged with maintaining a semblance of order in this untidy group. At the moment the only evidence of Josie McGee was an occasional flash of copper-colored curls in the midst of a writhing pile of uniformed youngsters.

There was no doubt about it, Cruz decided grimly. He certainly had his work cut out for him.

Then Cruz saw a familiar tousled blond head. Cruz blinked, not certain he believed what he was seeing. Billy?

The boy emerged from the wriggling knot, face shining with joy and perspiration, glasses askew. With a skinny index finger, Billy shoved the spectacles into place, then grabbed a handful of someone's shirt. The shirt's owner popped out of the mass.

As Cruz watched this strange child who was his son, Billy cupped his hands and whispered in the ear of a pudgy dark-haired boy. For several seconds the two youngsters shared their secret, then Billy covered his mouth and both boys burst into a renewed fit of giggles.

Cruz was stunned. Billy had always been a quiet child, painfully shy even with family and close friends. The boy had preferred books and computer games to rough-and-tumble antics of neighborhood kids. Cruz had accepted this, assuming that his son preferred the solace of his room over contact sports because Billy was more mature, more responsible than his peers. Besides, Catherine had been a quiet woman and Cruz always believed Billy had inherited his mother's understated personality.

But this . . . this was a side of Billy Cruz had never seen. He'd been a father for eleven years and he'd never even seen his own son involved in such childish horseplay. No, Cruz had been busy, too damned busy clawing for money and success to spend time with his own son. The realization hurt Cruz, and it humbled him.

Suddenly Billy looked up and saw his father. The transformation was startling. Billy's smile evaporated and his eyes grew wary. The boy stood quickly, awkwardly straightening his Scout bandanna as he walked stiffly to the nearest chair. Sitting quietly, Billy folded his hands in his lap and stared at the floor.

Cruz's shocked gaze was locked on his son, but he realized that all of the shouts had ebbed to hushed whispers. One by one, the other boys followed Billy's lead until the room was quiet and the entire troop was seated, tensely waiting.

A stinging prickle scratched Cruz's nape, a sick feeling of déjà vu. He remembered so many similar incidents over the years, times when Gunther Erickson had appeared and a happy room had fallen silent. Now it was happening again.

Only this time it was Cruz who had killed the laughter.

True to his word, Cruz was properly outfitted in official Scout leader garb. Obviously the man took his duties seriously.

Josie silently admitted that Cruz didn't look half-bad. On her, the uniform was like an ill-fitting Halloween costume. Cruz, however, with his broad shoulders and trim hips, looked like a soldier assigned to some elite special-forces unit.

Consoling herself that Boy Scout uniforms had not been designed to flatter the feminine form, Josie was still irritated that Cruz resembled a movie-screen sex symbol while she looked . . . well, she looked just plain silly.

Suppressing self-consciousness, Josie introduced Cruz to the troop. As each boy stood and offered the new leader a smart salute, Josie could almost see Cruz's brain turning. In fact she suddenly realized how the troop must appear to Cruz Erickson's fastidious eyes. It was not a pretty sight.

Although all the boys wore official uniform shirts, most preferred blue jeans to the tailored Scout slacks. Few wore hats, as modern hairstyles didn't accommodate the snappy red berets.

Richard Foster, for instance, had a cylindrical flat-topped cut that rose from his skull like a fuzzy eraser. Richard used his Scout neckerchief as a headband and looked disturbingly like a ghetto-gang refugee—which was exactly what he was. Considering what the kid had escaped, Josie wasn't about to nitpick about the boy's personal style.

Then there was Tran Nuygen, with his suspicious black eyes and swaggering manner, who would rather eat cactus than subject himself to something as wimpy as a funny hat and red scarf. Shaking a ragged thatch of stick-straight hair, Tran now folded his arms in subtle challenge. Josie noted that the gesture was not lost on Cruz, who met the boy's hostile gaze calmly before turning to the next Scout.

Donnie Kowolovich was a street-smart pseudo-surf bum with spiky blond hair and front teeth that would shame a gopher. Donnie's only concession to Scout tradition was the shirt. A red bandanna had been stuffed into his back pocket and torn canvas sneakers barely covered his sockless feet.

Of the entire troop, only Billy wore a complete crisply creased full-dress uniform.

Josie shifted nervously. She'd never insisted on spit-and-polish perfection, because each of the boys were new to Scouting. Some, like Donnie and Richard, came from families unable to afford the luxury of expensive Scout equipment. Josie had planned to move slowly, accommodating each boy's individual comfort level.

That these kids were even involved in Scouting was significant enough. They were misfits, youngsters unable to adapt to society's neat little norms. Josie wasn't about to estrange these boys for the benefit of conformity.

Still, she felt oddly distressed to realize how her beloved ragamuffins must appear to a stickler for perfection like Cruz. His silent disapproval spoke volumes. And it stung.

Ignoring Cruz's grim expression, Josie clapped her hands to gain the troop's attention.

"All right now, listen up," she said, then waited until the buzz of boyish chatter had subsided. "Let's get down to business. The Camporee isn't until August. That gives us almost three months to decide what, if any, competitions to enter."

"How 'bout archery?" Richard suggested. "I got a bow for Christmas."

Donnie made a rude noise. "No, man. It's gotta be something we can all do."

"Does not."

"Does too."

As the argument grew more raucous, Josie slipped two fingers in her mouth and emitted a piercing whistle. Cruz jumped as though shot. The room fell silent as eight expectant faces turned her way. Josie glanced at Cruz from the corner of her eye. He'd been quiet throughout most of the meeting, but Josie took no comfort in that, certain that the condition was merely temporary.

She was right. Cruz cleared his throat.

Here it comes, she concluded bleakly. Swallowing uncharitable thoughts, she politely turned toward him. "Do you have a question?"

He looked awkward, charmingly so. As he tugged at the collar of his brand-new khaki shirt, Josie found the nervous gesture rather endearing.

"I'm not familiar with this . . . Camporee," Cruz finally said. "Exactly what is it?"

"All the troops in the Orange County region will converge for a three-day camp-out at one of the local parks," Josie explained. "It's an annual tradition."

"And these 'competitions'?" Cruz's eyes gleamed.

Josie didn't like that. She squirmed. "Well, there are various events scheduled—races, ball games, even knot-tying and such."

"Ah." Cruz smiled smugly. "That's wonderful. We'll enter them all. What's more, we'll win."

"Pardon me?" Josie felt a slow heat rising. "I believe the question of events has yet to be decided."

Cruz frowned and Josie knew with leaden certainty that the war had just begun.

Unfortunately she was right. For the next thirty minutes, the entire troop engaged in a raucous discussion of being the best, working the hardest, ad nauseam. Cruz manipulated the aspects of troop pride and challenging odds to overcome adversity. His heartfelt analogy of "The Little Engine that Could" had Josie rolling her eyes.

Josie countered that the boys should have fun, pointing out how many nights and weekends of practice would be required to prepare for the myriad events.

As the argument heated up, it became clear that the troop was pretty evenly divided on the issue, with one small exception: Billy. He seemed miserable, eyes cast downward, not adding a single suggestion to the melee.

This entire situation was out of hand, Josie decided. Who the devil did Cruz Erickson think he was, waltzing in and taking over like this? The more forcefully Cruz pushed his own point of view, the angrier Josie became. Finally she'd had enough.

Standing, Josie forced a killing smile and spoke through clamped teeth. "I'd like a word with you, Mr. Erickson. Outside."

It was time for the showdown.

Chapter Three

Who do you think you are—General Patton?'' Josie was angry enough to spit nails. Hands on hips, she hoisted herself up on tiptoe in a futile effort to appear more intimidating. It was foolishly like a blowfish swallowing hot air, but five-foot-four people facing six-foot-two people did such things. She glared up at Cruz. ''Who died and left you in charge of the world?''

Cruz scowled down at his feisty adversary. ''What's your problem? As I recall, my being here was *your* idea.''

''And not one of my better ones, I must admit. What were you trying to do in there—create havoc?''

''Havoc? Me?'' Cruz shook his head in disbelief and spoke to the heavens. ''This from a woman I found buried under a screaming heap of rowdy sixth-graders.''

Josie felt her skin heat. ''They were simply expending some pent-up energy. It makes them more attentive if they have a little playtime before the meeting.''

''Oh, yes. I found them quite attentive...when they weren't throwing spit-wads at each other.''

Be calm, McGee. Josie took a deep breath and suppressed the urge to climb his chest. "Let's discuss this rationally."

Skulking darkly, Cruz jammed his hands into his pockets. "That would be a refreshing change."

She swallowed a retort, then managed a stiff smile. "What we have here is simply a difference of opinion. Surely as two mature adults we can work this out to everyone's satisfaction."

Good. Calm and reasonable. Josie felt better already. "Now, it's obvious that a tiny troop of eight inexperienced boys couldn't possibly expect to enter thirty-odd events and hold their own, let alone win."

Cruz stared grimly at the ground, pushing a stone across the asphalt with the toe of his polished leather shoe.

Taking his silence as agreement, Josie relaxed slightly and continued to expound her logic. "The purpose of the Camporee is for the boys to have fun and to meet with other troops for a little R and R. Surely you can see why it's better for them to choose one or two events instead of pressuring the boys to be super-scouts."

Pursing his lips, Cruz seemed to consider this. Then he said, "No, I can't."

"You can't what."

"I can't see how letting them slack off and be lazy is better."

"Slack off?"

"Do you have a better expression for encouraging them to be losers?"

"Oh, for crying out loud—"

"Don't you realize how much pride and self-respect those kids would have if they came out on top, as winners and champs?"

Josie was shaking. "And what if they lose? How much damage would *that* do to their collective little psyche if they feel their self-respect is dependent on some stupid contest?"

Cruz's jaw convulsed in tiny spasms and his eyes flashed angrily. "Dammit, *life* is a 'stupid contest' and these boys have to compete to survive. We have an opportunity here to teach them the discipline and moral values to grow into fine proud men."

"They have a lifetime for that," Josie snapped. "Let them be kids, for heaven's sake. They have a right to their childhood. They'll grow up soon enough—everyone does."

"Not everyone, it seems." Cruz folded his arms tightly and gazed across the darkened playground. His eyes stopped, focusing in the distance. Josie turned and saw that he was staring at the silhouette of her motorcycle, parked alongside the gymnasium.

Determined not to disclose how his words had stung, Josie knotted her hands together and spoke quietly. "I'm quite aware that your opinion of me is less than sterling, but—"

Cruz interrupted, surprising her as he cupped her chin and tilted her head back. Josie saw real emotion in his dark eyes and heard a faint tremor in his voice. "My remark was uncalled for. I apologize."

Well. That unexpected reversal left Josie a bit unnerved. She could deal with anger and indignation. She could even deal with blatant disapproval, but she was having considerable difficulty in dealing with the pain she saw in Cruz's eyes, and the regret in his voice.

She'd seen that same pain in his eyes earlier, as he'd stood in the doorway watching Billy play. Afterward Cruz had made an extreme effort to be jovial, to put the boys at ease. Josie had noted and appreciated that effort. In fact she'd been touched by it. She hadn't expected a man with Cruz's rigid perspective to put himself out so that children might feel more comfortable, yet he had done just that. The man was an enigma.

And he was very, very close.

Her chin still rested on the pad of his finger and his thumb caressed her cheek with the delicacy of a fleeting breeze. There was new warmth in his eyes, a sensual awareness glowing in the amber depths. Her pulse fluttered, her chest tightened, her lips fell apart in unconscious invitation.

She was overwhelmed by his nearness, by the spicy maleness scenting the night air. His free hand slid up her arm and her skin tingled beneath his warm touch. Heat radiated through her shoulder, then around her back as he urged her closer, and closer still, until her own hands rested limply against his large chest.

If he kissed her she'd be doomed.

Josie knew that as surely as she'd known anything in her life. There was something mystical about this man and the power he held over her senses. Josie felt suddenly defenseless, like that once-sad, wise-eyed child caught in the grip of something greater than herself. Josie was afraid and fear gave her sudden strength.

Pushing away, she turned shakily and took a deep ragged breath. What was wrong with her, anyway? A man's touch had never paralyzed her limbs and emptied her mind. She'd always been immune to this kind of thing.

Josie rubbed her eyelids. It must be the uniform, she mused silently. After all, women were supposed to be suckers for men in uniform, weren't they? Perhaps she'd simply fallen victim to the subliminal message of that trite cliché.

As Josie recovered her mental balance, Cruz shook himself from a bewildering trance and wondered what sinister force had taken hold of him. Demonic possession was the only answer, because Cruz realized that he'd damn near made a pass at his son's Scout leader.

Was he losing his mind?

So what if the woman had lips made for a man's mouth? Who cared if her eyes glowed with sensual promise and her sultry voice turned masculine brains into oatmeal? He could handle it. To Cruz, self-discipline was more than mere virtue; it was a way of life. Even this brief lapse was enough to confuse him. Confusion annoyed Cruz and annoyance made him irritable.

"So," he muttered grumpily, "the bottom line is that you don't want those kids to grow up." Cruz saw Josie's shoulders heave as she took another deep breath. He suppressed an urge to gather her in his arms.

"Perhaps that's true in a way, but there are things you aren't aware of," she replied softly.

"What 'things'?"

Turning, she faced him with an expression of sadness that touched Cruz to his very core.

"Some of these boys have a pretty tough home life," Josie told him quietly. "For instance, Donnie works in his father's restaurant after school and weekends. I had to talk myself blue just to get his parents to allow him a few days off once in a while for troop meetings and outings."

Cruz didn't see that as particularly tragic. "I had a part-time job when I was ten. It's good experience."

"I don't disagree in theory, but sometimes it goes too far. Donnie works until nine every night. He does his homework in the restaurant kitchen, trying to study between loads of dirty dishes. His sister was forced to drop out of high school and work to help support the family."

"That's child abuse," Cruz pronounced. "There are child labor laws—"

She held up her hand, stopping him. "I know, but Donnie's family is from another culture. They don't see it that way and, besides, the children have been raised to take on such responsibilities almost from the cradle."

Even in the darkness, Cruz could see Josie's eyes plead for understanding. She continued, her voice thick with emotion. "There are so many kids like Donnie, kids who have been forced to grow up too fast, kids with old eyes who have forgotten what it's like to be children. I just want them to have a few fleeting hours to remember, to have fun."

Something twisted inside Cruz. Josie spoke eloquently on behalf of her young charges, but there was more to her heartfelt words than lip service. Cruz knew that he'd seen a hint of something buried deep within Josie McGee. Her pain was very real—and very personal. Someone had hurt her, and for a blinding instant, Cruz felt a primitive surge of fury toward anyone who had caused her sorrow. He wanted to protect her. He wanted to take her in his arms and—

Cruz shook himself. It was happening again. Somehow this small curly-headed sprite had burrowed inside him and was taking over. He didn't understand what was happening, why this woman affected him so deeply. He was confused, annoyed and irritated.

He shielded his heart with tightly crossed arms. "That's all well and good, but fun isn't a license for irresponsibility." As usual Cruz masked conflicting emotions with a rigid expression and authoritative tone.

But Josie saw only an intractable man, unfeeling and unyielding, self-assured to the point of arrogance. "I give up. You're impossible." Josie threw her hands up to emphasize her frustration, spun on her heel and stomped across the playground.

She stopped twenty feet from Cruz and stood fuming in the darkness. This wouldn't help, she realized. At this point, she and Cruz were behaving worse than the boys. Good grief, the man could certainly push her buttons. No one had ever sent Josie's blood pressure so high, so fast. Billy's father did strange things to Josie's heart-rate, too, and she was beginning to wonder if her physiological reactions were due purely to anger.

Of course they were, she told herself firmly. This man was infuriating enough to make a nun cuss.

Still, he'd been right about one thing: this *had* been her idea. Josie hadn't a clue as to how to make this unfortunate situation workable.

At that moment her mental sojourn was interrupted by a loud crash in the gymnasium, followed by the screech of angry young voices. She sprinted toward the open door, aware that Cruz was right behind her. When they dashed into the room Josie sucked in a quick breath. Two of the boys were struggling in a combat that appeared to be more of a hugging match than a fist fight, but the youngsters were obviously not feeling particularly affectionate. Chairs had been overturned and the rest of the troop surrounded the small warriors, cheering and hollering encouragement.

The smaller boy dug in, lowering his head and pushing himself forward until his opponent made a whooshing sound and fell over backward. Before Josie could close her sagging jaw and react, Cruz had crossed the room and snagged the smaller boy, lifting him by his belt. The startled boy folded and dangled from Cruz's strong hand like a limp towel.

Then Cruz hauled the second Scout up by the scruff of his neck and set both boys upright with enough force to rattle them. The youngsters took one look at Cruz's grim face and snapped to attention. The room fell silent.

Josie emerged from her shocked trance. "What on earth—" Her voice had risen to an annoying squeak, so she cleared her throat, clamped her jaw tightly and spoke through her teeth. "What is going on here?"

Each boy pointed to the other and two voices chimed, "He started it."

Cruz took one step forward, stopping as Donnie stepped from the cheering section. Ignoring Cruz, he turned to Josie. "It wasn't nothing."

Josie's gaze swept over the solemn group. "I'm very disappointed in all of you." Heads drooped under the sting of her disapproval; the boys fidgeted, eyes cast downward.

Donnie shuffled awkwardly, then mumbled, "We were just trying to fix things."

Josie frowned. "What things?"

With a shrug, Donnie stared at the floor, then slanted a glance first at Cruz, then back at Josie. "You guys were fighting and stuff. Richard was saying we should win everything and be champs and stuff, but Tran said that was bull— Uh, I mean, he said it was bunk and so, well..." Donnie's voice trailed off and he stepped back into the anonymity of the group.

Josie felt like someone had kicked her in the stomach. Cruz had gone totally ashen. Cruz and Josie had just given the entire troop a rousing demonstration of how fine upstanding mature adult people settle quarrels. The boys had learned quickly.

But it was Billy who brought the lesson home. Instead of joining the fracas, he'd hung back in the farthest corner, watching in absolute horror. Now he ran to Cruz, pulling his father's arm with wet imploring eyes. "Let's go home, Dad . . . please. I don't want to come back. I don't want to be a Scout anymore." A tear slid down Billy's cheek.

When Cruz looked at Josie their eyes locked in silent communication. No words were needed. If the two of them couldn't resolve their differences both knew that the troop would disintegrate.

Neither would allow that to happen.

The following evening, Cruz sat stiffly on Josie's sofa and nervously smoothed the rumpled slipcover. He slanted a glance toward the kitchen just as Josie fumbled, splashing iced tea across the counter. Frustrated, she muttered to herself and roughly sponged up the mess. Cruz was relieved to realize that she, too, was feeling a bit jumpy.

Last night he and Josie had made a pledge, to themselves and to the boys, that by the next meeting all disagreement would be resolved. Then the troop could race forward, gears meshing, engine humming like a well-oiled human machine.

Tonight was the first step. They'd spend the entire evening together—the entire night, if necessary—and they would find a solution.

Tonight. Together. Alone.

This Scout business had definite potential, Cruz mused, casting another furtive glace at his hostess.

As usual, Josie was dressed casually, but jeans and a T-shirt had never seemed so provocative. Cruz tried to look away but couldn't quite manage that. A man would have to be brain dead not to notice how her breasts moved beneath that soft cotton top, or how the denim cradled her swaying hips.

Cruz wiped his damp forehead. Lord, it was hot in here. He wished Josie would hurry with that iced tea.

As though clairvoyant, Josie called, "It's almost ready," then arranged cookies on a small tray. The grouping didn't look quite right, so she fiddled with the pile to create a more appetizing display. It didn't help.

From the corner of her eye, Josie saw Cruz fidgeting and recognized her delaying tactic. Still, she nervously adjusted and readjusted the tiny pile of iced squares.

Josie felt as if she was about to jump out of her skin. She didn't really know why she was so darned edgy, but she knew that *he* had done this to her. There was something about the man that activated every one of her warning alarms. Perhaps it was his commanding presence that unnerved her, or his muscular shoulders or his soft brown eyes and kissable mouth . . .

Oh, good grief.

Josie rolled her eyes and moaned. She was hopeless. Put her in a room with an attractive man and suddenly she was sweating like a sex-starved spinster. Ridiculous, utterly ridiculous. Obviously this ludicrous situation was affecting her physically, but Josie could handle it.

She was in complete control—pure thoughts, clear mind, strong body.

Josie silently repeated that phrase like a mantra, rearranging cookies until she felt her breathing deepen and her pulse slow. There. She was fine now, absolutely great. Mind over matter and all that.

Smiling, she carefully placed two frosty glasses on the tray, totally calm, totally in control.

Then the parrot squawked a rude suggestion and Josie nearly dropped the tray. Whirling, she shoved a finger in the startled bird's face and snarled, "Keep your beak shut, buster, or I'll pluck you balder than a Thanksgiving turkey. Got that?"

Alarmed, Walter screeched and flapped his wings.

Cruz straightened, grinned and began to applaud.

Josie squeezed her eyelids together and wished she could simply disappear. So much for cool and calm. All she could do at this point was smile and pretend that she always threatened her bird.

Somehow Josie managed to set the refreshments on the coffee table and seat herself primly beside Cruz. They smiled politely, munched tasteless cookies and sipped their tea.

Finally Cruz broke the silence. "We made a real mess of things last night, didn't we?"

Nodding, Josie set her glass on the table. "I'd say so."

"Do you have any ideas?"

"I have plenty of ideas. Unfortunately you don't seem to care for any of them."

Cruz frowned. "With that attitude, we're not going to get anywhere."

Josie bristled. "Are you saying that this is all *my* fault?"

"Let's just say that you've made a major contribution."

Josie stood, glowering down at him. "From my perspective, there weren't any problems until you stuck your pompous nose in my business and—"

Cruz rose up like an angry phoenix. *"Pompous?"*

"Yes, pompous." Her chin jutted defiantly. "And self-righteous and judgmental and . . . and . . ." The words dissipated.

At the same moment, each realized what was happening. They were at it again. Suddenly the entire situation seemed just too idiotic. They were worse than the boys, two adults who couldn't say three words to each other without verbal combat. It was all so . . . silly.

Cruz's eyes gleamed. Josie bit her lip. Cruz's shoulders started to vibrate. Josie's mouth twitched.

Then they both lost it. Laughter burst forth, drowning anger, healing secret wounds. They let the sweet mirth take over, howling until tears and hiccups had them gasping for breath.

"I-I'm sorry," Josie finally stammered, wiping her face. "I honestly don't know what's come over me lately. I'm usually more laid-back."

"I know what you mean. Billy says I've been acting pretty weird myself—says I should 'chill out.'" Cruz fell back against the sofa and shook his head. He closed his eyes, smiling contentedly. "Maybe we see each other as some kind of threat."

Josie's head snapped around. "Threat? How could I possibly be a threat to you?"

One brown eye opened. "Billy likes you."

She pursed her lips and tried to grasp the significance of that strange statement.

Cruz sat up and rubbed his neck. "Billy and I have been alone for so long it was kind of frightening when he suddenly started with Josie-said-this and Josie-said-that. It was almost as though—" Struggling for words, Cruz finally gave up. He couldn't express what he didn't completely understand.

But Josie nodded as though he'd given an eloquent soliloquy. "You must have felt as though you were losing him."

Surprised, Cruz met her direct stare and saw compassion. Josie laid a soft hand on his knee and said, "You and Billy have been very close, haven't you?"

"Yes." Cruz's chest constricted as though squeezed by giant hands, and the hot lump in his throat made his voice raspy. "Billy's mother died five years ago. He misses her."

"And so do you." It wasn't a question, but to Josie's surprise, Cruz took it as one and answered.

"Sometimes," he acknowledged. "I wish I'd given Catherine more. She was so quiet and accepting that I often wonder if she was truly happy."

"I'm sure she loved you very much."

Cruz's smile was a little sad. "In her way, she did. But we were so young when we married—she'd never had a chance to find herself, to know what she really wanted."

"If she hadn't wanted to marry you, she wouldn't have."

"I'm not certain she had all that much choice. Neither did I actually. Our families had been close for years and it was simply assumed that we'd marry someday." Cruz tried to lighten the mood with a tense smile. "Fortunately, we liked each other and had quite a bit in common."

Josie didn't know what to say, so she said nothing. Arranged marriages in this day and age? It seemed positively archaic.

Leaning back, Cruz laced his fingers behind his head, lost in sad memories. "After Billy was born, I got my first big promotion. From then on it seemed I was always at the office or on a plane to somewhere. I was in Boston when Catherine had her first stroke and by the time I got a plane home, she'd had a second and was dying."

"I-I'm so sorry. That must have been very difficult for you."

Cruz closed his eyes. "It was worse for Billy. Because I had been away so much my son and I were almost strangers. I've tried to make it up to him but he still spends more time with his grandmother than he does with me."

"Why is that?"

"Being successful is a full-time job," Cruz said with a subtle hint of rancor. "I refuse to travel now but there still isn't enough time."

Josie considered this. "Your career must be very important to you."

"It's a living."

"There are less-stressful ways to make a living," Josie pointed out.

"Perhaps, but it would be a tremendous blow to my family if I gave up the trappings of success." Cruz saw Josie's arched brow and added, "I have responsibilities to my parents, as well as to my son."

"Quite a juggling act."

His lips tightened. "That it is. Unforunately I seem to be dropping the ball lately and my son is the one who is suffering."

Josie found the entire conversation to be disconcerting. She was surprised that Cruz had shared such personal insights with her, but was absolutely stunned to realize that a man who appeared so confident would have secret gnawing doubts. Cruz was apparently unsure of his parental abilities and after five years still looked back at his marriage and wondered if he'd been wrong.

Josie was touched by his admission and the vulnerability it revealed. This was not, she realized, an unfeeling or callous man. Cruz Erickson cared deeply for people and had apparently spent much of his life trying to please them.

She felt a warmth rise up inside and a burning need to offer comfort. She laid her hand gently on his sleeve. "Being a single parent is rough, but you've done a wonderful job. From what Billy has told me you've never made him feel unwanted or resented."

Cruz was shocked by her words. "How could parents resent their own child?"

Shrugging, she simply said, "Some do."

She spoke calmly, but with a subtle authority that gave a sense that her words came from personal experience. Cruz wondered about that and phrased his next question carefully. "Do you have children?"

Eyes widening in surprise, Josie replied, "No. Why do you ask?"

"Well, it just seemed as though..." Cruz squirmed uncomfortably. "I mean, you spoke as if you'd had some experience with single parenthood."

Her hazel eyes reflected both amusement and understanding. She smiled. "I have, but from the other side. My mother was never married."

"Never?" Cruz's jaw dropped comically.

"It *does* happen."

"Yes, well, of course it does. It's just that I hadn't realized that you were..."

"Unpedigreed?" Josie's eyes twinkled with mischief but Cruz looked so ill at ease she decided to let him off the hook. "It doesn't bother me, really. Lena and I both survived the experience. She's still living in Texas, but we keep in touch."

"Is Lena your sister?"

"I'm an only child. Lena is my mother." Josie found herself grimacing at the thought of siblings. Josie'd had her hands full taking care of one irresponsible mother, thank you very much. At any rate, Josie found the discussion distasteful and tried to distract Cruz. "Shall I freshen your tea?"

"It's fine, thanks. Why do you call your mother by her first name?"

"That was her preference. How about another cookie?"

Cruz rejected the offer with a wave of his hand and zeroed in on the subject. "That seems a rather unusual preference."

"Well, Lena is a rather unusual person." That was certainly an understatement, Josie thought. Lena was one of a kind and that was fortunate. The world simply wasn't ready for more than one.

This entire conversation was disquieting, but Josie took one look at Cruz's grim expression and realized he wasn't ready to let go. She sighed. He had, after all, trusted her enough to bare his soul. They were going to be working together and the more they knew about each other the easier it would be to establish a solid working relationship.

She took a deep breath and looked Cruz in the eye. "My mother wanted me to use her first name so that her dates wouldn't know she was old enough to have a daughter my age."

Cruz did a double take. "Pardon me?"

Josie shrugged. "Lena liked men and she liked to have fun. Having a child around the house put a damper on both, so she told everyone I was her kid sister."

"And people actually believed that?"

"Sure." Josie laughed dryly. "If you knew her, you'd believe it, too. At twenty-six, she looked and acted like a teenager. She drank too much, partied too hard and had absolutely lousy judgment when it came to boyfriends. If I had a nickel for every time I thought she'd been killed by one of the louts I'd be a rich woman."

"My God," Cruz whispered.

Glancing up, Josie saw his expression flicker from disbelief to absolute horror. She'd said too much and could have bitten off her own tongue. All she could do now was try to soften the impact. "It wasn't all that bad," she added hastily. "Some of her friends were really quite nice." And some of them weren't. Josie pushed away the unpleasant memories and forced a smile.

"These, ah, friends—did they live with you?"

"Some did." But never for long. One thing Josie had learned early in life was that men, even the kind ones, were merely transient entities. Eventually they always left. In the end a woman had only herself to depend on. It wasn't good or bad; it was simply the way things were.

Josie realized that Cruz was speaking and dragged her mind back to the present. "I'm sorry, what did you say?"

"I asked who took care of you."

"I took care of myself." Josie stiffened at the pity she saw in his eyes. "The world is filled with latchkey kids, so I'm not exactly an anomaly."

Cruz looked away. "I didn't mean to hurt you."

"You didn't," she snapped, too quickly. "I mean, all kids have to do chores and homework, things like that. I may have had a bit more responsibility than most, but that doesn't make me an abused child."

"Is that all that was expected of you—homework and a few household chores?"

Now Josie looked away. The conversation was hitting too close to home and Cruz's knowing words had pierced her deeply. Lips tightened into a thin line, Josie clenched her fists and fought the rush of memories. She squeezed her eyelids shut, forcing the images away, willing her thoughts away from the past. It was over. Nothing could be gained by reliving the pain, remembering the filthy neighborhood and the tiny trailer where she'd once lived. All through her childhood, Josie had seen eyes filled with pity and disgust.

Poor and trashy, they'd called her. *The whore's kid.*

Lena hadn't been a prostitute; she'd simply been scared and lonely, with a woman's body and the mind of a child. Like all people, Lena had wanted to be loved, but had been naïve in pursuit of that coveted emotion. People with puritanical small-town mentalities hadn't cared much about facts. Anyone less privileged than themselves was to reviled, shunned by the self-righteous and the judgmental.

Josie had been ashamed of her mother and of herself. But over the years she'd managed to overcome most of those early emotional traumas.

Josie McGee was a survivor.

Chapter Four

"Josie?" Cruz's voice urged her softly.

"Ummm?" She stared into thin air.

"I asked if anything else had been . . . expected of you."

Her response was so soft he hardly heard. "No, nothing."

Deep down Cruz knew that wasn't completely true. Something had wounded her, scarred her. Inadvertently Josie had given him an insight into her past, a hint of why she so passionately defended the children of today. But it was too vague, too ambiguous for Cruz to file in his neatly organized mind. The mystery nagged him and Cruz knew he'd find the answers. He had to. Josie McGee was making him crazy.

Cruz saw Josie's eyes grow distant, then flicker with remembered pain. He felt an ache like a dull-toothed saw ripping his innards. Beneath Josie's facade of determination and self-sufficiency beat a fragile heart. He saw vestiges of the frightened child she must once have been, and the exposed vulnerability made him want to fight the world for her.

His own reaction was shocking. Compassion wasn't a foreign emotion for Cruz, but these feelings went beyond that. Suddenly he felt connected with her, an intimate emotional bonding so intense it was almost spiritual. Josie had hold of an obscure part of Cruz.

But this was preposterous. Cruz mentally shook himself. Josie McGee was only a woman, and if truth be told, she was a rather bizarre one at that. She talked to parrots. She rode an enormous motorcycle and wore black leather. To complete the bohemian image, the woman bounded around with all manner of feathers and beads and shiny metallic shapes dangling from her shapely earlobes.

Josie McGee was an enigma. She was playful and compassionate, yet she was also quarrelsome and a bit prickly. Cruz could live with that. What unnerved him most was her fearless defiance, the way she challenged life to a duel of fate. Cruz admired her spunk but was appalled by conduct he perceived as brash and reckless.

Still, he suspected that Josie's audacious attitude was rooted somewhere in her mysterious past. She was a woman with a secret that clouded her eyes with vague sadness and inexplicable fear. Cruz was determined to lift that veil and relieve her inner suffering. At the moment he didn't have the vaguest notion of how that could be accomplished, but he was compelled to do something, anything to relight the laughter in her eyes.

Only as a friend, of course.

Cruz had met many attractive and exciting women. He appreciated beauty, but was searching for something deeper, something solid. An adventurous unpredictable maverick like Josie had no permanent place in Cruz's traditional life. His brain knew that; all he had to do now was to convince the rest of his body.

Josie blinked as though awakening from a trance, then fidgeted uncomfortably. Forcing a starched smile, she looked straight at Cruz. "Let's get on to the subject at hand, shall we?" The question was rhetorical and she hurried on with strained cheeriness. "We've only got a few weeks until the Camporee and the troop bank account is in bad shape."

"How bad?" Cruz asked, then winced at the answer. "Sounds like a fund-raiser is in order."

"Exactly." Standing, Josie went to the kitchen and dug through a cluttered drawer. "I went to the local chamber of commerce meeting last week with a poignant plea. Granger's Market came through with some groceries and The SportsPlace donated a propane cook stove. I wrote everything down—aha!" Triumphantly she pulled out a rumpled sheet of yellow lined paper and scanned it. "All in all, not too bad for a fifteen-minute speech, even if I did have to squeeze out a tear or two."

Plopping back on the sofa, she thrust the paper at Cruz, who was having a bit of trouble keeping up with her sudden burst of energy. He focused on the list as Josie continued chattering. "As you can see we're still going to be short of supplies. Some of the boys don't have sleeping bags or tents or—"

Cruz interrupted, pointing to a scrawl on the paper. "What does this mean—'gas station, Saturday'?"

Josie squinted at the line in question. "Oh, the Thrifty Gas over on Oak Street is letting us hold a car-wash fund-raiser."

Scowling, Cruz muttered, "I've never heard of such a thing."

"Really? You *have* led a sheltered life." Josie ignored Cruz's dark look. "Basically the boys will all meet at the station first thing Saturday morning armed with buckets and rags. Then we'll set up signs on Oak to bring in customers. I figured we can handle about six cars an hour at three dollars each. With two five-hour shifts, we'll have a hundred and eighty bucks in the kitty."

Cruz stared. "Have the boys ever done this before?"

"Not that I know of."

"Then what makes you think they even know how to properly wash a car?"

"What's to know? You soap the dumb thing up, then squirt it off. I hardly think they'll need a Ph.D to handle that."

"What about vacuuming the inside? Or polishing the chrome? The windows need special solutions or they'll streak—did you get donations for that, too? And what about liability insurance? If a car is damaged, we could be sued. What if we don't even have enough customers to cover the cost of the supplies?"

Josie's head was swimming under Cruz's rapid-fire questions. She went from startled to confused to downright agitated. "This is a troop fund-raiser, not a corporate takeover."

"Still, we have to approach this in a professional manner. It's our responsibility to analyze risks and weigh the options—"

"Oh, good grief." Standing, Josie rubbed her head, then locked her hands behind her back and paced. "Do you have to be so darned fussy about everything? The cleaning supplies are going to be donated and the Boy Scouts of America are an incorporated nonprofit entity that has met all insurance requirements of the state." Whirling, she folded her arms and glared at him. "Now unless you have something better in mind—"

"As a matter of fact I do." Cruz's smile was a bit too smug for Josie's liking. "Supporting the troop should be the boys' responsibility. They should elect a fund-raising chairman from their own ranks. You've been all over town, running yourself ragged to take care of everything. The boys will have learned nothing more than to sit back and reap the benefit of someone else's effort. Besides, once the initial windfall is gone, the troop will be right back in the same boat—broke and looking for someone to bail them out."

The logic startled Josie. Cruz's point was well-taken and she slid him a wary glance. "Exactly what are you suggesting?"

"A recycling program." Leaning forward, Cruz's voice hummed with enthusiasm. "The boys could collect aluminum, paper and bottles. It would be an ongoing process and their success would be in direct proportion to the amount of effort expended."

Josie's breath slid out between slack lips. "It would take weeks, maybe months to put such a program into operation."

Cruz agreed. "Nothing worth having comes easy. It's time the boys learned that."

"But what about Camporee? We need money now."

Shrugging, Cruz said, "Initially, they may have to do without and make some sacrifices. That's part of the lesson."

Disbelief soon turned to anger and Josie's vision of eight disappointed children overshadowed the deeper message in Cruz's rationale. She had promised the boys that she'd find a way to get them the money and equipment they needed. No way was she going back on that promise.

"I won't let them down," she said firmly. "Whether you like it or not, the car wash is on."

"Now wait a minute—"

"End of discussion." Josie pirouetted and marched into the kitchen. As was her habit during trying times, she poured cleanser into the sparkling clean sink and began to scrub.

The sofa springs squeaked and Cruz's determined footsteps followed her. When he spoke, Josie recognized the tight tone and knew without looking that the funny little muscle in his jaw was twitching wildly.

He bit off the words. "This discussion will end when we both agree that it's over and not one second earlier."

"It takes two people for a discussion." Bubbles oozed between her knuckles as she concentrated on her pointless task. "I'm through talking."

"Then you can just listen—and stop scouring that damned sink." Grasping her shoulders, Cruz whirled Josie around until they stood toe to toe. Her eyes first widened, then narrowed dangerously as Cruz continued his authoritative diatribe. "The purpose of this evening was to come to some kind of agreement about the troop. I'm not leaving until we've done just that."

"The sofa is a bit lumpy, but if that's what you want, I can probably hunt up a blanket for you."

They glared at each other, then Cruz tightened his grip on her shoulders. "The first thing I want is to know why you're so determined to have everything your own way," he growled.

That got her attention. "Me? You're the one who's trying to shove your ideas down everyone's throat, no matter who gets hurt."

"Who's going to get hurt?" He seemed sincerely perplexed by the suggestion. "What's wrong with planning ahead and involving the boys in deciding their own future?"

Bitng her lip, Josie's gaze lowered. "Nothing is wrong with that."

"Then what's the problem?"

She watched foaming bubbles drip from the sponge in her hand to the waxed linoleum. "The boys have been looking forward to the Camporee and I promised that somehow I'd get them there."

"I don't want them to be disappointed, either, but it's more important that they understand their own responsibilities. If they want it badly enough, they'll work for it."

"They're just kids. You expect too much of them."

"Do you really believe that?"

"Yes." She looked him in the eye. "Yes, I do."

Cruz shook his head. The woman was driving him nuts. Releasing Josie, he speared his fingers through his hair and turned away. "So we have another stalemate," he muttered. "Where do we go from here?"

Josie leaned weakly against the sink and tried to shrug off the pleasant tingling sensation his touch had caused. She dropped the sponge on the counter and sighed. "I don't know."

The entire situation seemed impossible. Josie and Cruz couldn't spend two minutes in the same room without arguing, yet the future of the troop depended on resolving differences and working together. At the moment that seemed unlikely.

As Josie considered the dilemma, a scraping sound caught her attention. Walter cocked his head cautiously and continued shuffling sideways along his perch. The bird had been uncharacteristically quiet throughout the discussion and Josie absently wondered if her scolding had anything to do with this subdued mood. She felt guilty. After all, it certainly wasn't Walter's fault that Cruz Erickson was so darned bullheaded.

And sexy.

Cruz suddenly threw up his hands, muttered something unintelligible and marched back into the living room. Before Josie could react a loud thud was followed by an outraged male bellow.

"Line drive!" Walter screeched hysterically.

Lurching around the corner, Josie found Cruz sprawled on the floor, swearing colorfully, holding the basketball that had apparently rolled from the corner into his path.

"Are you all right?" she asked.

Cruz pushed a wavy strand of blond hair from his forehead and stared up grimly. "Do I look all right?"

Actually he looked absolutely devastating, but Josie swallowed the impulse to tell him so. Instead, she took the basketball, tucked it under her arm, then stretched out a hand to help him up. "I . . . uh, I'm sorry."

His eyes began to twinkle. "Tell it to my lawyer," he said casually, then grasped her hand and pulled.

But instead of Cruz coming up, Josie went down, falling across his lap. The basketball bounced free and rolled away. Shocked, Josie gasped and twisted until she was lying in Cruz's arms like a surrendering lover. The position was far too erotic to be comfortable, and far too comfortable to be safe.

Cruz's arms tightened. One of Josie's hands was resting against Cruz's chest and she realized that her other hand was sliding across his back as though she'd lost control of the appendage. Nervously Josie licked her lips and felt Cruz's abdomen tighten. His body was rock hard, yet quivered beneath her touch in tiny spasms, which were strangely arousing.

Physically Cruz was perfect and she yearned to run her palms across every rippling inch of him. Josie had never before wanted to touch a man in such an intimate manner, but now she actually craved the feel of his bare skin next to hers.

Josie's hands trembled and her mind fogged with burgeoning desire far beyond her experience. Without conscious thought of consequence, Josie brushed her fingertips across the sculpted contours of his upper body.

Cruz sucked in a rasping breath and uttered a small groan, which sent shards of electricity racing down her spine. Then she heard a soft contented sigh and realized that the sound had come from her.

Deep in her passion-fogged brain, alarm bells were jangling. Josie was in deep trouble and the worst part was that she didn't give a hoot. All she wanted was to feel Cruz's strong mouth on her lips, feel his soft hair tangled in her fingers. All she wanted was to make love with him—now, here, forever.

And she just might have done so, if Walter hadn't chosen that moment to shriek, "Low and inside...awwrk...hit the showers!"

Bolting upright, Josie shoved a thick mass of curls from her forehead. Cruz seemed to be in shock, as though he, too, was realizing how close they'd come to initiating a significant change in their relationship.

Dazed, he watched Josie scramble to her feet and awkwardly smooth her rumpled shirt. Cruz shook his head as though clearing mental cobwebs, then mumbled a garbled apology.

"No problem," Josie croaked.

Cruz stood slowly, offering a sheepish grin. "At least we weren't arguing."

Josie felt her face heat. "We weren't solving anything, either."

Sobering, Cruz rubbed the back of his neck. "No, we weren't solving anything."

He bent to pick up the errant basketball, handing it to Josie. Then an idea struck her. She bounced the ball on the carpet, mulled the thought over, then slanted a glance up at Cruz. "Are you a betting man, Mr. Erickson?"

Cruz was instantly wary. "That depends."

"I have a proposition for you—winner takes all."

Cruz cocked his head and his mouth twitched. "Sounds provocative. What did you have in mind?"

Her gaze skimmed over him. She noted broad shoulders and saw muscular thighs straining beneath stylish safari pants. Powerful, Josie decided, but probably not too quick on his feet. There was no doubt about it. She could take him.

She smiled sweetly. "Do you play basketball?"

Sally's jaw sagged comically as she leaned across Josie's desk. "*You lost?* The woman who held her own in an exhibition game with the Harlem Globetrotters lost to a pinstriped desk jockey? I don't believe it."

Josie swallowed hard, folded her hands primly on the dented desktop and tried to maintain her composure. "I didn't lose," she said forcefully. "We played off time limits and it was a tie."

Waving off that information as irrelevant, Sally snorted. "Same thing."

"No, it's not the same thing at all." Hands flat on the desk, Josie stood and leaned over until her nose was even with Sally's. "The car wash is still scheduled for Saturday, so I got exactly what I wanted."

One of Sally's sparse eyebrows hitched wickedly. "And what did *he* get?"

"Nothing particularly perverse." Josie smiled, noting Sally's obvious disappointment. "Actually everything has worked out rather well. The car wash will bring in enough money for the Camporee and the recycling program will put some money in the bank for next year."

Sally frowned. "That all sounds terribly reasonable. Why on earth did you have to go to the mat on it?"

Shrugging, Josie sat down and shuffled papers. She couldn't answer her friend's question. Sally was right; the compromise *had* been terribly reasonable, but when Josie and Cruz were in the same room "reasonable" flew out the window.

Then Cruz's words echoed in Josie's mind. "Maybe we see each other as some kind of threat," she mused aloud. Seeing Sally's confusion, Josie elaborated, "Cruz said that when Billy began to talk about the troop—and about me, well, he felt a bit left out, that's all."

"He said that?" Sally whistled. "I'm impressed."

"Why would that impress you?"

"Because there aren't too many men in the world who would admit such unmacho feelings." Sally plopped on a nearby chair. "So why do you feel threatened, Josie?"

"I don't." Her response was too sharp. "I mean, I don't think that I do. It's just that Cruz is so strict with Billy and he expects so much from the boy. He's so... so..."

"Gorgeous"

In spite of herself, Josie smiled and nodded. "That, too."

Sally laughed. "Now that makes sense, especially for a woman like you."

"What do you mean by that?"

"I've known you for three years, Josie McGee, and in all that time, you've never once given the slightest hint of being attracted to a man." She wagged a finger in Josie's startled face. "Honestly, I've been a bit worried about you. It's one thing to assert your independence and quite another to carve out a life of spinsterhood."

"I'm not trying to assert anything," Josie protested.

"Don't get me wrong," Sally said soothingly. "I'm not criticizing. After all the years you spent mothering your own mother it's perfectly normal to avoid the dependence of another human being. But there's a big difference between sharing and controlling, you know."

Josie's chin snapped up. "Are you saying that I control people?"

"Absolutely not." Sally emphasized the statement with a vehement shake of her head. "But you seem terrified of *being* controlled, sometimes to the point of being obstinate."

"That's absurd." Josie's denial was weak and her brain was churning. It wasn't absurd at all, she realized. Josie had made a career out of dealing with people successfully, yet she had been stubborn and unyielding with Cruz Erickson. Why? At first, she'd thought him to be the kind of parent who views his child as property, an extension of his own desires. She now realized that her initial judgment had been flawed. Although Josie didn't agree with many of Cruz's parental philosophies, she knew he was a fine man with high morals and a deep love for his son.

But Cruz brought out strange feelings in Josie, feelings she'd never experienced and felt powerless to control. That frightened her.

That threatened her.

Before Josie could fully absorb the implications of this revelation, a chaotic din of angry voices filtered from the outside playground. Standing, Josie saw Sally run to the window, then mutter under her breath.

"It's those blasted troublemakers again," Sally said. "Shall I call the cops?"

Moaning, Josie shook her head. "Not yet. Let me see if I work something out with them."

Sally understood. Both women had been through this before. The group in question, a half-dozen juvenile thugs known as the Boogaloo Blasters, seemed to get a perverse thrill out of terrorizing the younger kids. Josie had frequently confronted the leader, a cowardly braggart named Turk.

Josie suspected that Turk and his friends were simply bored and neglected, getting attention in any manner that worked. During the gang's last appearance, they'd eventually swaggered off with blustered threats and rude hand gestures. This time, Josie would try to involve them in playground activities, give them a sense that they, too, were entitled to a few hours of fun and recreation.

But first she'd have to frisk them for weapons.

Pausing in the doorway, Josie called over her shoulder to Sally. "Stay here and watch out the window. If things get out of hand, call in reinforcements."

Cruz rolled down the car window, allowing the spring air to ruffle his hair. The warm breeze felt wonderful and even though six reports and a departmental budget sat on his desk awaiting approval, the paperwork could grow moss for all he cared. Birds were singing, the sun was shining and the day was just too wonderful to spend in a dreary office. Besides, Josie would be off duty in a few minutes and he wanted to see her.

To talk about the boys, naturally.

And to watch how delightfully her cheeks dimpled when she laughed.

Cruz frowned and reminded himself that he and Josie were merely colleagues. Oh, there was a certain attraction between them, no doubt about it, but these things could be controlled. He and Josie McGee were too different to be anything other than good friends.

Weren't they?

Of course they were.

Frustrated, Cruz steered into the recreation center parking lot. What was he doing here, anyway? He had responsibilities waiting for him back at the office and yet here he was, planning a leisurely afternoon with the beautiful woman whose image had invaded his every waking moment.

As Cruz sat in his sensible four-door sedan, he relaxed. What the hell, he told himself. As Josie would say, a little R and R never hurt anyone.

With that, a smiling Cruz exited the car and promptly froze in his tracks.

Across the graying asphalt was a sight that made his pulse leap and his breath catch in his throat. It was Josie, and she was completely surrounded by a scruffy gang of teenaged hooligans.

Cruz felt his lungs constrict in fear. There were at least five brutes—draped in chains and torn leather adorned by skull-and-crossbones insignia. The group advanced ominously, closing around Josie.

One of them had a knife.

Cruz couldn't believe what he was seeing. Head back, hands on hips, Josie was defiantly challenging a dangerous thug twice her size. She ignored the glinting small blade as though it were nothing more than a harmless shiny bauble.

Cruz was appalled. Cruz was terrified. In one instant Josie's life could be snuffed out like a candle in the rain. Life was fragile and death came quickly, without warning, without cure.

Long ago Cruz had learned that painful lesson. His brother had once been laughing and alive, a flesh-and-blood existence that had been wiped out in a single heartbeat. Ray was gone. Regrets couldn't bring him back; nothing could. Death allowed no second chance.

And there was Josie, fearlessly perched on the precipice of forever. Cruz didn't think. He reacted.

In less than a minute Cruz bolted across the parking lot and levered a headlock on the startled ruffian.

"Drop it," Cruz growled savagely and was rewarded by the clatter of metal on pavement.

Josie watched Cruz's melodramatic entrance in a state of shock. "Cruz, what in the world—"

"Go inside," Cruz snapped. "I'll take care of this."

Josie stiffened at his commanding tone, but was still somewhat numbed by this baffling turn of events. Before she could open her mouth again, Cruz secured Turk's arm with a deft twist. The movement yanked Turk's cronies from their momentary stupor.

One boy reached into his jacket. From the corner of her eye, Josie caught the movement and whirled around. "Don't even think about it," she warned. With a snarl the kid whipped out a weapon and before Cruz could move, Josie aimed at the teenager's wrist, then disarmed him with a stinging roundhouse kick.

Satisfied, she silently thanked her karate teacher, then turned on Cruz. "Let go of him."

Frowning, Cruz stared in confusion.

At the moment, Josie was in no mood to be polite. She had just spent ten grueling minutes convincing Turk that there was more to be gained by being a part of the program than by constantly trying to thwart it. In fact, Turk had just agreed to allow Josie to hold the gang's weapons in return for use of the basketball court when Cruz had suddenly appeared like some kind of avenging Rambo and snared the poor guy by the throat.

Josie was angry and humiliated. "I said, *let go of him*,"

Reluctantly Cruz complied. Turk emitted a string of obscenities, rubbing his neck as he snatched up the fallen knife. Cruz made a move toward the re-armed boy and Josie instantly stepped between them.

She spoke to Turk. "I'm sorry about this. Obviously, Mr. Erickson misunderstood the situation."

Cruz's jaw dropped. "This thug had a knife on you."

Tiredly Josie shook her head. "No, he was giving me the knife to hold so they could use the facilities."

Turk stuck out his beefy chest. "Forget it, dude. This place stinks." With that, Turk spun on his heel and stomped across the yard. His friends followed, turning occasionally to shout insults until the entire gaggle of Boogaloo Blasters had disappeared behind the building.

Josie skewered Cruz with narrowed eyes. "Well, quite a smooth show you put on. Do you do this kind of thing often?"

"Do you?" Cruz replied harshly. "I thought you spent your days directing youngsters to the nearest rest room. It never occurred to me that you enjoyed playing chicken with armed hooligans."

Cruz was agitated. He seemed overly upset by the incident and Josie could only watch in stunned silence.

"I should have known," he ranted, pacing with stilted steps. "I should have realized that you were into self-destruction the minute I saw you riding that damned death machine." He spun and faced her. "What the hell is wrong with you, anyway? Are you strictly out for thrills, no matter who gets hurt? Don't you care if you kill yourself and leave the people who love you to grieve the rest of their lives?"

When Cruz finally stopped raving, he was shaking and breathing hard. Josie saw his eyes focus on her, then register surprise. She was bewildered by Cruz's behavior but was beginning to suspect that the knife incident had triggered some kind of dormant fear. It was as though Cruz concealed some secret wound that had been unexpectedly ripped open to expose a raw pain, one that Josie recognized, but didn't yet understand.

Something, or someone, had hurt Cruz. His torment touched her deeply. Josie had the impulse to hug him and erase the horror she'd seen flash through his eyes.

Reaching out, Josie softly caressed his face. "Why are you so frightened?" she whispered and felt his jaw pulsate.

Cruz turned away, mumbling something Josie couldn't quite hear. When he faced her again, he was composed, although obviously still shaken.

"I may have overreacted," he acknowledged stiffly.

Stung by the sudden coolness of his voice, Josie pulled her hand away. She cleared her throat. "No apology is required."

"I'm not apologizing." Cruz seemed offended. "It was obvious that you needed assistance whether your ego allows you to admit that or not."

Josie snapped, stung by his rebuff and angered by his superior tone. Her sharp words sliced like Turk's blade. "I had the situation under control. I've been working for months to bring those boys into the mainstream and in one macho moment you ruined everything." Cruz's eyes widened and his chin sagged. She continued, ignoring his stunned expression. "Why in the world did you feel as though you had to muscle in like some kind of protective grizzly, anyway?"

A red flush crept up Cruz's neck. "I thought he was going to... hurt you."

Josie softened. "I know, but I can take care of myself."

"Can you?" Their eyes met, held for a moment, then Cruz sighed. "Yes, I suppose you can."

He looked bewildered, hurt and for some strange reason, rejected. Josie didn't understand. She wondered if someone else had refused Cruz's protection and if that refusal had resulted in tragedy. His wife, perhaps? No, that didn't seem likely. Cruz's wife had died of a stroke—or at least, that's what he had told Josie.

Still, Cruz had this enormous sense of duty toward everyone around him. Josie had seen proof of that in the way he guided his son and the manner in which he spoke of family responsibility. In fact it was amazing that Cruz's poor shoulders were still so straight with all the burdens he'd piled on himself. And there was something else Josie had noted in Cruz's eyes, something that made no sense at all. When he'd been pacing and ranting, Josie had seen fear in his eyes, but she'd also seen shame.

Cruz shuffled and jammed his hands into his pockets. His face was rigid but his eyes were like those of a lost puppy. He stared over Josie's head and spoke to the clouds. "I'm taking Billy to the carnival over at the fairgrounds tonight."

Folding her arms, Josie studied the pavement. "That should be fun."

"Would you like to join us? If you have no other plans, that is."

Surprised, Josie looked up and saw Cruz watching her anxiously. He managed a tight smile and added, "It'll give us a chance to talk... about the troop, of course."

It would also give Josie a chance to dig a bit deeper into Cruz Erickson's stoic psyche. The man fascinated her, but given her background in psychology such interest was to be expected. It was purely professional. Well, mostly professional. There were, she silently acknowledged, other facets of the man that affected her on a more primal level. But she could control those feelings; she always had.

Chapter Five

Maybe it was the full moon. Then again, it could have been the soft spring air giving the night such a mystical quality. Whatever it was, Josie didn't want to waste time analyzing. The evening had been too wonderful.

Everything had started normally enough. Cruz and Josie had disagreed as to whether cotton candy or licorice was worse for one's teeth. Since no basketball courts had been handy, the dispute was solved when Billy flipped a coin. Licorice won.

Cruz had begun the carnival adventure much like a tolerant tour guide, pointing out the most appealing attractions, then smiling benignly as Josie and Billy attacked ferris wheels and shooting galleries with equal enthusiasm. Soon, however, Josie had noticed a change. Cruz had joined in, reluctantly at first, then with all the zeal and intensity one could expect of a dedicated successful executive.

Most executives, however, wouldn't leap on a carousel horse hollering, "John Wayne, eat your heart out!"

Josie loved it. Billy loved it. And the crowd . . . well, the applause said it all.

Now Josie leaned against the counter of a booth and watched Cruz try to win a sad-eyed goldfish by tossing a Ping-Pong ball into its bowl. The outlook was not good. Ball after ball bounced off the rim. Cruz scrunched his forehead in steely determination; Billy poked his glasses into place and cheered encouragement. The final ball ricocheted from the fishbowl and landed in a startled woman's soft-drink cup.

Cruz mumbled repeated apologies as he mopped the woman's arm with a soggy tissue. Josie stuffed a fist against her mouth and swallowed her laughter.

As the indignant lady disappeared into the crowd, Billy patted his father's shoulder. "That's okay, Dad. I don't need a goldfish."

"Of course you do," Cruz replied with mock dismay. "Look at the poor thing. What do you see?"

Billy looked at the fish. The fish looked at Billy. "I see an orange fish with black spots," Billy said.

"A *disappointed* orange fish with black spots," Cruz corrected.

Josie snickered. "I didn't realize fish were capable of disappointment."

Cruz appeared offended. "They have feelings, you know."

Josie smothered a smile. "Of course. How insensitive of me."

Placated, Cruz turned to the burly booth operator. "How much for the fish?"

"Three balls for fifty cents," the man replied, scratching himself.

"I don't want to throw any more balls at it. I simply want to buy it."

The man's tiny eyes gleamed and he looked at Cruz as though the word *sucker* had suddenly appeared on Cruz's forehead. "Well, I ain't supposed to just sell 'em, you know.

But seeing as you'd give it a good home and all..." He paused, glancing around to assure that no eavesdroppers lurked nearby, then straightened and grinned. "Ten bucks."

"What? I could buy an aquarium full of fish for that."

The big man shrugged and the negotiation went into full swing. Shaking her head, Josie could only watch in total amazement. Before her very eyes Cruz had metamorphosed from a hard-shell chrysalis into a free-spirited fun-loving butterfly. And she liked the transformation.

The fish discussion, however, was apparently going to be a bit long-winded for her taste, so she bent and whispered into Billy's ear, "Let's go watch the go-carts."

Billy's eyes lit like neon. "Neat!"

They got Cruz's attention long enough to tell him where they'd be, then headed across the fairgrounds to the large oval track where a number of miniature race cars zoomed around an obstacle course rimmed with strategically placed tires. Billy was enraptured by the tiny machines, climbing on the railing for a better look.

"Wow," he murmured. "Look at the red one. It's totally rad."

"It's a good-looking car," Josie agreed, smiling at Billy's wistful expression. "Would you like to take a turn?"

His head snapped around, eyes wide and hopeful. "Do you think I could?"

"I don't see why not. The sign says that you have to be forty inches tall and I'd say that qualifies you."

Billy's grin widened, then dissipated. "I don't think Dad will let me."

"Nonsense. He's let you go on all the other rides, hasn't he?"

"Yeah, but..." His voice trailed off and he looked back at the shiny little car as it pulled into the pit area.

The boy looked so pitiful it tugged at Josie's heart. She put her arm around his thin shoulder. "You run over and claim that car. Your father should be here any minute, and as soon as he gives the okay, you can hop in and show those slowpokes what a *real* driver can do."

Billy smiled gratefully, then dashed away to implement the plan. As Josie had predicted, Cruz appeared a few minutes later balancing a bowl that sloshed at every step and contained one bored-looking goldfish.

Holding up his prize, Cruz grinned and ignored the water dripping down his elbow. "Got him," he announced smugly.

"I had no doubt you would," Josie replied . "You can be very persuasive."

Cruz looked pleased.

"What did you finally agree to pay?"

His smile faded. "Well, price wasn't really the object here. I mean, look at the quality of this goldfish."

The fish looked like a sushi reject to Josie. She eyed Cruz suspiciously. "You didn't give that awful man ten dollars, did you?"

"Well, no." Cruz swallowed. "The bowl was an extra five."

Josie stared for a moment, then burst into laughter. The man had definitely gone over the edge, and it was the funniest thing she'd heard all day.

Cruz resolutely allowed her a few moments of mirth, then changed the subject. "Where's Billy?" he asked, glancing around.

Choking, Josie wiped her eyes and waved a hand in the direction of the pit. "Over there. He's waiting his turn."

Frowning, Cruz looked toward a mob of youngsters, searching for a familiar blond head. "Waiting his turn on what?"

"The track. He's really got his heart set on driving that little red go-cart."

Cruz felt a tightening in his chest. With increasing urgency he scanned the crowd. Then he saw Billy, stroking the fender of a tiny red car. Cruz felt sick. His skin turned cold and icy perspiration beaded his upper lip. Suddenly his mind warped back in time, to an image from the past so vivid he seemed to relive the moment.

Ray had touched a red car with the same loving strokes, and Cruz remembered every detail of one long-ago night.

After the argument with Gunther, Ray had concealed the car at a friend's house. That night Cruz had sneaked out, following his brother on a secret mission. From behind a fence, Cruz had watched with awestruck ten-year-old eyes as Ray had talked to an older boy. Then Ray had looked up, spotting Cruz. At first, Cruz had been afraid his brother would be angry, but Ray had just grinned and waved him over.

"Hey man, she's a beaut, isn't she?" Ray had puffed with pride. "And she's all mine—lock, stock and dual carbs."

"Wow," Cruz murmured, stunned by the beauty of the shiny machine. "Did Dad say you could keep it?"

Ray sobered. "I've been saving for two years. It's my money and it's my car. He's got nothing to do with it."

To Cruz, defying their powerful father was right up there with facing a nest of spitting machine guns, and at that moment Cruz thought his big brother was the bravest person in the world. "Dad's going to be awfully mad when he finds out," Cruz warned.

"He's not going to find out." Ray's eyes turned cold when he added, "Unless you tell him."

"I wouldn't," Cruz protested. "Honest."

Then Ray grinned. "Then this will be our secret, okay?"

And Cruz had felt ten feet tall to realize that the powerful older brother whom he so fervently admired was actually depending on him.

"I'll never tell," Cruz promised vehemently. "I'd rather die."

Die. I'd rather die.

Now, images flashed through Cruz's brain, blurred yet terrifying, a film caught in fast forward as he mentally fumbled for the off switch. In his mind, Cruz saw Ray's red car, a scarlet streak speeding through an open white tunnel an instant before the stenciled flame had lit the night sky.

Cruz was horrified by the startling image. What did it mean? Why did he feel as though someone had reached into his body and yanked out a vital organ?

Nothing made sense at the moment. Ray had died in an accident. Cruz remembered his parents breaking the news without details and to this day Cruz had never sought out the particulars. It was enough that Ray was gone. Cruz never wanted to know how it had happened.

"Cruz... what is it?" The feminine voice brought Cruz back to the present and he was aware of Josie beside him, clutching his arm.

Roughly he shook her off. "Get Billy," Cruz commanded. "It's time to go."

"But he's next in line—"

"No!" Cruz spun so quickly that water sloshed from the fishbowl. "No cars, is that clear?"

Josie backed off, watching the disturbing change with confusion and concern. "It's very clear, Cruz."

Josie saw Cruz's expression flicker from terror to shock, as though he'd suddenly realized the impact of his words. Cruz reached out in a conciliatory gesture, then his hand dropped heavily to his side. His eyes held the deepest pain Josie had ever seen. Then Cruz turned and quietly walked away.

Saturday was clear and warm, a perfect day to get wet. Josie loaded her bike's storage compartment with neatly folded rags, then roped a stack of borrowed buckets to the sissy bar and roared out of her driveway.

When she veered into the Thrifty Gas, she saw three of the boys unpacking the trunk of Cruz's car. Cruz looked up, wincing in disapproval until Josie had parked the bellowing machine and turned off the shuddering engine. Slinging her helmet over the handlebar, Josie proceeded to untie her cargo. She heard Cruz walk up behind her.

"Let me help," he said quietly.

She stood back. "Thanks."

He frowned and tugged at the knots. "It would be a lot easier if you'd trade this monstrosity in for a station wagon."

"I'd rather run barefoot on barbed wire than sell Sylvester," Josie replied, wrinkling her nose. When she rubbed her hand lovingly over the gleaming black body, Cruz flinched. Josie saw something startling in his expression. It was that same sudden and inexplicable fear.

Then Cruz quickly looked away, concentrating on the task of unloading car-wash supplies. Remnants of his personal torment were revealed only by his tight mouth and wary eyes. Josie wondered what demons held silent vigil in his mind.

She remembered that haunted expression from the carnival. One moment Cruz had been laughing and happy, then without warning, his eyes had glazed with secret terror. Afterward Cruz had been subdued and somber, but when he'd called Josie yesterday, the carnival incident had been ignored. It was apparent that he didn't want to discuss it; still, Josie wondered.

There was something about Cruz's sadness that touched Josie deeply. She felt helpless, yet wanted desperately to erase the hurt from his eyes. The feelings Cruz invoked in her were unexpected and surprisingly intense. She was mentally musing the implications of those feelings when Cruz's voice jarred her. She blinked at him. "Pardon me?"

"I said, let's get this show on the road," Cruz muttered grimly, then hefted a stack of buckets and strode toward the waiting group of Scouts.

Grabbing an armful of rags, Josie followed. Troop 161's first major fund-raiser was officially under way.

The next two hours were a bit of a blur. They had more customers than anticipated, and by ten o'clock cars were lined up throughout the large parking lot. An emergency phone call brought three obliging parents and a couple of commandeered siblings, but by lunch time the entire group was exhausted to the point of being punchy.

In spite of the dizzying pace, Josie noticed that both Cruz and Billy seemed tense. When she saw Billy take a break she handed her drying cloth to the nearest scout and followed. She found Billy crouched beside the garage, looking unhappy.

"Hard work, huh?" Josie sat beside Billy, who nodded glumly. "Is something on your mind? You seem a bit distracted."

The boy shrugged, then slid a covert glance toward Cruz, who was engrossed in polishing a windshield.

Josie followed Billy's gaze. "Did you and your father have an argument?"

"Not really." Billy stared at the asphalt, tracing the outline of an oil stain with his finger. "It's just that..." His voice trailed away.

"Just what?" Josie prodded gently.

Billy sighed. "I flunked a science test yesterday."

"I see. And your father is angry with you?"

"No. Dad doesn't get mad. He just gets...disappointed."

Josie nodded knowingly. "I can see why you'd feel badly about that, but I'm sure he understands that these things happen."

"But it was my fault," Billy whispered. "I told Dad that I was studying but—" he swallowed "—I was practicing square knots and stuff."

"Ah. Well, we all make mistakes." Josie hugged her knees. The poor kid already knew he'd blown it—no sense making him feel worse.

But Billy needed to excuse his failure. "It's just that I always have homework and I just get sick of it, you know? It's important for kids to have fun and stuff—you always say so."

Josie felt like she'd been punched. Tripped up by her own philosophy. Again. Of course, Billy had twisted her words a bit to fit more neatly into his own cause; still, she realized that she had some responsibility to clarify this matter.

With a deep breath, she slid an arm around Billy's shoulders. "Fun *is* important but so is schoolwork. There has to be balance and everyone has responsibilities, Billy, even kids. The most important responsibility you have at this stage in your life is to get an education. This is something that you have to do for yourself—no one can shove knowledge into your brain. You have to seek it out, work for it. Then it's time for fun. Do you understand that?"

Contrite, Billy nodded, peered up at Josie, then beyond. His eyes widened.

Turning, Josie saw what had startled Billy. Not ten feet away Cruz stood watching quizzically. He'd obviously overheard the last part of their conversation and Josie's muscles stiffened.

Cruz smiled, focusing on Billy. "Break's over, son. You're needed in the suds section."

Billy scrambled to his feet and loped across the parking lot.

Cruz saw Josie's wary expression before she stood and dusted off her jeans. Before he could say how impressed he'd been with the way she'd handled Billy, she slid him a guarded look, mumbled something about getting back to work and scurried off.

Leaning against the stucco garage wall, Cruz watched as Josie joined the washers. The woman constantly surprised him. He wouldn't have expected her to support his position on the homework issue. Heaven knows, Josie seemed to have a real fetish about children being overworked; yet, she did indeed have a sense of priority that wasn't so different from his own. Perhaps he'd misjudged her.

The realization was disconcerting. Cruz knew that if it hadn't been necessary to deal with Josie McGee, he would have written her off as shallow and self-indulgent.

And look at what he would have missed.

* * *

Josie had suds hanging from her earrings. Donnie was soaked to the skin and the rest of the troop was operating under the impression that wetter was better. Only Billy was relatively dry, performing his duties with optimum caution.

Cruz had noticed his son's reluctance to join the festivities with the same joyous abandon as his troopmates. As a matter of fact, Cruz had noticed a great many things in the past couple of weeks. Billy seemed unable to cut loose like the other boys and Cruz blamed himself, recognizing that his son was emulating his own rigid demeanor.

That wasn't what Cruz wanted for Billy. In fact it wasn't even what Cruz wanted for himself. Meeting Josie McGee had been like looking in a mirror for the very first time. In that undistorted reflection, Cruz had seen his own father's face.

The revelation had shocked Cruz to the core.

The cycle of guilt and intimidation had been handed from father to son for untold generations, but that unhealthy sequence must be broken. This was a good time to start, but how? Certainly a lecture on the merits of playful behavior would appear more as criticism than encouragement. Of course, one could always fall back on the old adage that actions speak louder than words.

Yes, indeed, Cruz decided. *Action it is.*

Josie glanced up and instantly knew something odd was happening. Eyes twinkling, Cruz was stalking Billy, concealing a hose behind his back. Fascinated, she ignored the suds dripping off her face and watched as Cruz prowled circles around his confused son.

Cruz smirked. "I've noticed something rather upsetting," he said silkily. "You're the only dry Scout in the pack."

Billy's eyes widened. "S-so?"

"So that could only mean one thing," Cruz announced. "You're not working hard enough."

Before the startled boy could respond, Cruz leveled the hose on him and twisted the nozzle. Water sprayed out like a geyser. Billy shrieked and dashed away, giggling madly. Cruz chased him and the rest of the boys cheered.

Josie closed her mouth and swallowed hard. She'd seen Cruz watching Billy with a variety of expressions: sadness, determination and, finally, total mischief. Suddenly she realized what this display was all about. Cruz had seen Billy's caution, his reluctance to risk parental disapproval by doing something messy or, heaven forbid, childish.

Apparently Cruz realized how he'd contributed to Billy's fear. In the only way he could, Cruz was showing his son that it was okay to be a kid. It was okay to have fun.

Josie was impressed. It had never occurred to her that a man like Cruz Erickson would even acknowledge his own shortcomings, let alone make a determined effort to overcome them. With every day that passed, it was becoming more obvious that he was doing just that and Josie admired him immensely.

Still, such an important lesson should be left half learned. Crouching, Josie grabbed a nearby bucket and stealthily advanced. When she was close behind the laughing duo, she stood, holding the bucket in a ready position. "Billy isn't the only one who has managed to stay dry," she purred.

When Cruz turned, he received the full force of soapy water at midchest. His arms flew out like flapping wings. The hose hung limply from one hand, harmlessly spraying thin air. He looked as shocked as if he'd spotted his own mother moonlighting as a go-go dancer.

Josie gasped, choked back a howl of laughter, then saw that Cruz's shock had worn off a bit too quickly. His eyes gleamed and with a deft flick of his wrist, the hose was pointing right at her. She would have hollered, except if she'd opened her mouth she might have drowned on the spot. Helplessly she sputtered and tried to protect herself with her arms.

Then the entire troop emitted a simultaneous war cry and leapt into the fracas. Josie opened one eye just as Cruz dove forward, grabbing her around the waist and wrestling her to the ground. She tried to protest but was laughing too hard to do anything besides emit a wet unladylike gurgle.

Cruz's mouth rested on her ear. "So you want to play rough, do you?"

Trying to catch her breath, she vehemently shook her head. "N-no, honestly..." She looked into his face and was racked by giggles. "You have suds on your nose."

He grinned wickedly. "Does that excite you?"

Actually it did. She sobered and squirmed beneath him. "Not at all," she managed in a strained voice.

"Then you must be cold," he said, suddenly hoarse. His eyes were drawn to her wet T-shirt. He swallowed hard, then met her gaze. She saw passion in his eyes, and desire. It shocked her. It shocked him.

Immediately he rolled off her and stood, coughing uncomfortably before extending his hand to help her up. They shuffled awkwardly, taking deep breaths, composing themselves, ignoring each other and the watery chaos exploding around them.

Finally Cruz cleared his throat, grabbed a hose from the nearest exuberant Scout and spoke loudly enough to be heard over the din. "That's enough, guys. Back to work."

Slowly the excited group calmed, then ambled back to the business at hand. Everyone, that is, except Josie. She stood as though rooted, her hand clutching her throat, trying desperately to forget the feel of Cruz's hard body pressing against her.

Things were getting complicated.

A small bonfire flickered in a ring of stone. Excited young voices floated through salty air as the ocean alternately sighed and rushed like great heaving breaths. Moonlight illuminated concealing clouds with a silvery glow, which shimmered across the inky water.

It was a picture-perfect night, but Josie was too distracted to appreciate its beauty. Her emotions were in chaos. Sensations flooded her like cresting waves. She was confused and felt as powerless to control her feelings as the sand was powerless to control the raging surf.

Josie sat quietly, arms wrapped around her knees, bare toes burrowed in sand. The beach party had been her idea, a way to reward the boys for a good day's work at the car wash. At the moment, however, she wished that she'd given them all a hearty handshake and sent them home. Then she wouldn't be staring across flickering flames noticing the way firelight made Cruz's hair glow like a golden halo.

Now she was waxing poetic. Great. All Josie needed was a case of "romantic moonlightitis." Maybe penicillin would help.

As Josie cogitated about her ill-timed malady, a small hand thrust something grossly black and wrinkled in front of her face. "Want a hot dog?" Donnie asked.

She nearly gagged. "No. . . thank you."

Donnie shrugged, bit the end off the horrid-looking object and sauntered away.

Josie returned her gaze to Cruz. This time, however, he was watching her, too; staring actually, with an expression hot enough to rival the fire. Their eyes met and held. His gaze was as tangible as a touch and just as arousing. Josie knew she should look away but couldn't. She felt mesmerized, a prisoner of her own escalating emotions. The man had a Svengali-like effect on her mind and his mere presence made her hormones vibrate. Heat was buildng deep in her very core, then washing outward with the rhythm of a warm tide.

She wanted him.

The realization shocked Josie from her trance. Shakily she pulled her gaze away and stared over the black water. This would never do, she told herself firmly. At twenty-six, Josie was well beyond adolescent crushes and swooning hero-worship. Whatever she was feeling now was strange, she silently acknowledged, but she rejected the notion that such emotions were uncontrollable. It would simply take a bit of self-discipline, and in spite of Cruz's opinion to the contrary, Josie had plenty of that.

Admirable qualities aside, Cruz Erickson was still a man. Josie knew about men. Scooping up a handful of warm sand, Josie watched the tiny grains run through her fingers. Men were like sand, she mused. On the surface, they felt warm and solid and permanent, but if one tried to grab hold, they simply slipped away.

Josie had learned that lesson. Lena hadn't.

Allowing her thoughts to travel back in time, Josie remembered the tiny trailer of her childhood. Masculine faces flashed through her mind, faces of men who had, for better or worse, left an indelible mark on Josie's life.

Through the years, Lena had brought home a variety of men. Some had stayed for a while; most hadn't. Josie had pretty much ignored them all, until Paul McGowen had appeared like a smiling god.

Little Josie had believed Paul the answer to her childish prayers. Paul had been kind and caring, loving and strong. In Josie's young eyes, Paul became the father she'd never had. With him, Josie discovered bedtime stories and zoos and picnics in the park. He taught her how to be a child and Josie loved him for it.

Whenever Lena retreated to bed with the "sickness" of too much booze, Paul had been there to hold Josie and murmur comforting words. He'd said it wasn't Josie's fault that her mother drank. Paul had never condemned Lena, seeming to recognize the illness. But he'd also been Josie's defender and white knight, arguing that Lena expected too much of a child.

Josie had adored Paul and called him Daddy. He'd been the only man to stay longer than a few weeks. She loved him, and deep in her little-girl heart, she'd foolishly believed Paul would always be there.

Then came the night Josie had awakened to Lena's shrill shrieks and Paul's quiet determined voice. A cold pit had opened in Josie's stomach. She'd climbed out of bed, silently praying it wasn't happening again—not with Paul, not with Daddy.

Please God, don't take my Daddy away from me. I'll be a good girl—I'll be the best little girl in the whole world, only please don't take him away.

Now, sixteen years later, Josie could still remember Paul's taut face. In her nightmares, she saw the telltale suitcase in the same strong hands that had been so comforting. Josie remembered the hot sting of tears as she'd thrown herself against him, clinging and sobbing, begging Daddy not to leave her.

"I'll be better," Josie had cried desperately. "I'll clean the floors every single day and I'll never burn your shirts with the iron and I'll be so good, you'll be proud of me and . . ." She'd choked on the words because Paul had lifted her into his arms and kissed her cheek so sweetly.

"My darling Josie," he'd whispered. "I *am* proud of you."

"Don't go away, Daddy," Josie had sobbed. "Don't leave me."

"I have to go, precious. I've tried, because I love you so much, but things between your mother and me have just gone too far. None of this is your fault, sweetheart. Remember, I love you."

Then Paul had turned away and, prying Josie's tiny fingers from his legs, he had simply walked out of her life.

It had been a heartbreaking lesson, but one thoroughly learned. Over the years Josie had never forgotten what had been so painfully taught. Even good men were merely transient, making fine friends and good colleagues, but lousy lifemates. A woman must stand on her own, depend on herself. It had always been that way.

A childish wail of dismay broke into Josie's thoughts, transporting her back to the present. She looked quickly toward a distressed Scout. "What's wrong?"

"Mr. Erickson says we've got to go now," came the whining reply. "But there's still marshmallows left and it's really early."

Cruz picked up a limp cellophane bag. "Two squashed marshmallows does not a beach party make," he said firmly. "And I don't consider ten at night to be early. At least, not for a doddering old man like myself."

Startled, Josie looked at her watch. Where had the evening gone? Scrambling to her feet, she supported Cruz's position. "Mr. Erickson is right. Donnie, please douse the fire and, Tran, you make sure that all the trash has been picked up."

As Josie gave directions, she felt a sense of relief that this unnerving day was nearly over. Too much was going on inside her, a war of emotions that left her feeling drained. She needed to be home, needed to be alone to review all the prudent reasons for controlling one's fantasies.

Determined, Josie took a deep cleansing breath and started retrieving towels.

While the troop gathered its belongings, Cruz watched Josie and wondered why his throat felt like someone was squeezing from the inside. She looked like a lost child. During the evening, her expression had alternated from longing to surprise to fear and, finally, to sadness. She'd seemed light-years away. The experience had obviously been painful for her, and for Cruz, as well. He couldn't explain it, but her suffering cut through him like a razor. The urge to take her in his arms and caress away the hurt was almost overwhelming.

Cruz didn't understand this need deep inside him, this driving force that centered around Josie McGee. He couldn't keep his eyes off her; he couldn't keep his mind off her. And lately, thoughts of her had even invaded the sanctity of his dreams.

During the drive back, Cruz and Josie maintained their somber moods. By the time the final Scout had been delivered safely home, Billy had stretched out in the back seat and fallen fast asleep. The final blocks to Josie's house were driven in absolute silence.

Cruz pulled into her driveway and turned off the engine. They both sat quietly, staring sightlessly out the windshield. Finally Josie took a deep breath. She gave the door handle a savage yank, then leapt from the car before Cruz could react.

"Thanks for all your help today," she mumbled an instant before the passenger door swung shut.

The noise broke Cruz's trance. "Wait a minute." By the time Cruz extracted himself from the car, Josie was on the front porch fumbling with her keys. He caught up with her and saw her hands were shaking. "Are you ill?" His voice broke.

She shook her head. "Just tired, I guess."

Soberly nodding, Cruz shifted awkwardly. For some reason he didn't want her to disappear behind that damn door. "It was a successful day, don't you think?"

"Yes," she whispered, finally fitting the key into the lock.

He touched her wrist before she could turn the knob. He felt a bit desperate and more than slightly foolish, but simply couldn't help himself. The rigid, self-contained, always-in-control Cruz Erickson was suddenly stumbling like a schoolboy on a first date. But he was much too overwhelmed to be embarrassed. There was an urgency pressing him on, a desperation he couldn't understand.

He slid his palm from her wrist, covering her hand gently. Her skin was cold and he felt her tremble beneath his touch. She shivered, then reluctantly looked up. Her eyes were moist, reflecting his own confusion, his own turmoil. And his own desire.

When Josie finally met Cruz's gaze, she knew without doubt that her inner war had been lost. She saw wonder in his eyes and a gentleness so sweet that it melted the last vestige of her resolve. The man had touched her heart in a way she had never allowed and she felt helpless to stop it.

Cruz lowered his head, slowly, hesitantly, then paused as though awaiting rebuff. Head tilting back, Josie's lips parted in silent invitation. Even as Cruz's mouth grazed her cheek, Josie knew she should step away. She should muster the cool voice and chilling expression that had sent so many men scurrying for friendlier skies. But she couldn't. Her will was shackled by his gentle embrace and tender kisses.

Then his lips brushed hers, so softly it felt more like a breath than a touch. But the emotional jolt took them both by surprise. Cruz straightened, looking stunned. Josie clung to his arms, lips parted in shock, and felt as though his dark gaze was penetrating the secrets of her soul.

Cruz hesitated, then captured her mouth with a gentleness that soon grew more intimate, more demanding. Josie gave in to burgeoning desire, tangling her fingers in his hair, kissing him deeper and with more urgency than she'd ever thought possible.

Her insides rioted. Her mind was a blur. She was aware of nothing but Cruz's muscular chest pressing against her soft breasts, his mouth moving on her lips as he tasted and probed, possessing her completely.

The kiss ended. Josie moaned deep in her throat, a tiny whimper of regret. When she looked into Cruz's eyes, she realized just how deeply he was engrained in her heart.

And Josie knew without doubt that her life would never be the same.

Chapter Six

The blueprints spread across the drafting table had lain undisturbed for hours. To a casual observer, Cruz must have appeared totally dedicated, studying the plans with extraordinary care. In reality he didn't know if they were diagrams of a fuselage or an engine assembly. His concentration was focused on images of a curly-haired woman with huge hazel eyes and a defiant pointed chin.

Josie McGee was driving him mad. It had been nearly a week since the night they'd kissed each other senseless, and through the obscure days that had followed, Cruz had futilely tried to shake himself from his emotional stupor. It seemed a losing battle.

On the surface their relationship seemed calm and normal. The Wednesday troop meeting had gone smoothly, with final preparations being made for this weekend's campout. But Josie had been quiet and withdrawn, avoiding Cruz's eyes. Their conversations had been brief and limited to troop business.

ACCEPT FOUR BRAND NEW

YOURS

We'd like to send you four free Silhouette novels, worth $9.00, to introduce you to the benefits of the Silhouette Reader Service™. We hope your free books will convince you to subscribe, but that's up to you. Accepting them places you under no obligation to buy anything, but we hope you'll want to continue your membership in the Reader Service.

So unless we hear from you, once a month we'll send you six additional Silhouette Romance™ novels to read and enjoy. If you choose to keep them, you'll pay just $2.25* per volume. And there is *no* charge for delivery. There are *no* hidden extras! You may cancel at any time, for any reason, just by sending us a note or a shipping statement marked "cancel" or by returning any shipment of books to us at our cost. Either way the free books and gifts are yours to keep!

ALSO FREE!
VICTORIAN PICTURE FRAME

This lovely Victorian pewter-finish miniature is perfect for displaying a treasured photograph—and it's yours *absolutely free*—when you accept our no-risk offer.

Perfect for a treasured Photograph

Plus a FREE mystery Gift! follow instructions at right.

*Terms and prices subject to change without notice.
Sales taxes applicable in New York and Iowa.

WE EVEN PROVIDE FREE POSTAGE!

It costs you *nothing* to send for your free books — we've paid the postage on the attached reply card. And we'll pick up the postage on your shipment of free books and gifts, and also on any subsequent shipments of books, should you choose to become a subscriber. Unlike many book clubs, we charge *nothing* for postage and handling!

NO POSTAGE
NECESSARY
IF MAILED
IN THE
UNITED STATES

BUSINESS REPLY MAIL

FIRST CLASS PERMIT NO. 717 BUFFALO, NY

POSTAGE WILL BE PAID BY ADDRESSEE

Silhouette Reader Service™
P.O. BOX 1867
BUFFALO, NY 14240-9952

An intelligent man would recognize and respect so obvious a brush-off. But when it came to matters of the heart, Cruz was apparently not as intelligent as he'd once believed. He simply couldn't get Josie out of his mind.

The telephone rang and Cruz sighed, glancing at his watch. He assumed the call would be his boss inquiring about some past-due report. Lord knew there were enough to choose from. Cruz hadn't put in a decent day's work all week.

Grabbing the receiver, he curtly announced himself.

"Good morning. We missed you at dinner last night."

Isabel's soft voice filtered over the line and Cruz felt himself relax. "I'm sorry, Mother. Something came up."

"Ah." A small word, but Isabel gave it a knowing inflection. "Your father was disappointed."

Cruz massaged his forehead, feeling guilty. "I'll make it up to him."

The line was quiet for a moment, then Isabel said, "There were some important people that he wished for you to meet."

Guilt turned to annoyance. Cruz called himself seven kinds of a fool for not realizing that even a formal dinner party had ulterior motives. Gunther Erickson did nothing purely for recreation; business was always the underlying motivation.

"Apparently my father still isn't convinced that I have absolutely no desire to follow in his financial footsteps," Cruz said harshly. "I may never be as wealthy as he'd like, but I've chosen my career and I'm satisfied."

"Of course you are," Isabel soothed. "You have misunderstood your father's intention. He only wishes that you receive the recognition to which you are entitled."

Cruz rubbed his forehead and lowered his voice. "I'm not a child to be bullied into compliance. Those days are over."

Isabel sounded tired. "I know how frustrating it has been for you, *mi hijo*. But you must understand that your father means well and since Ramon—" Her voice caught and she struggled for control. Finally she simply said, "You are all he has left."

The conversational direction tightened Cruz's gut into a painful knot. "I realize that, but I can't bring Ray back and I can't spend the rest of my life trying to take his place."

"That was never expected of you." Isabel sounded stung and agitated by the accusation.

Cruz wished he could swallow his words, suppressing them in his subconscious where self-doubt had simmered for so many years. He didn't understand his own turmoil. Of course Cruz wasn't responsible for the fate of a brother seven years his senior. His own common sense confirmed that.

Still, something nagged Cruz. There were these peculiar images flooding his mind at the oddest moments, only to skitter away when he tried to pull them into focus. It seemed as though his subconscious mind was trying to communicate, knocking at a door Cruz was afraid to open.

He sighed, pushing the scattered blueprints away and leaning back in his swivel chair. Everything was getting too complex and unpleasantly cerebral. His neat methodical organized life was in disarray. Confusion irritated Cruz, and he was most definitely confused. Still, that was no reason to snap at the woman who had loved and supported him his entire life.

"I'm sorry. I shouldn't have said that."

Isabel spoke softly, without rancor. "Through all the years, you have done what was asked of you, and more. You are a perfect son, but such perfection can be frightening. When you were a boy, you behaved as a man. Sometimes I feared that..." Her words trailed away.

Cruz was alarmed by the emotion cracking his mother's voice. "What is it? What's wrong?"

Isabel was silent for several moments, although Cruz heard her breath catch softly in her throat. When she finally spoke, her voice was quiet but firm. "I loved your brother very much and when we lost him I thought I'd go mad with the grief—because I had lost both my sons that night."

An icy hand seemed to grab Cruz's spine. "What . . . do you mean?"

"You were my baby, Cruzito, a boy filled with love and with life," Isabel whispered. "When your brother died, the child in you died with him."

Cruz's fingers tightened around the receiver. Isabel's words opened the secret door to his mind.

In a flash of memories Cruz recalled raucous laughter and loud mufflers and shrill teenaged voices reverberating through a long-ago summer night.

"You can take him, Ray! Show him what you've got."

Cruz remembered the sickening sound of revving engines and squealing tires. He could almost taste the thick vile smoke and pungent gasoline fumes. He'd been nauseated by the smell and the secret terror. Dread and impending doom had blanketed the night like a shroud.

There had been a tearing crash, the din of smashing glass and grinding twisting metal. Then came a wailing anguished cry, a sound that tore at the soul and ripped through the blackness.

That tormented scream had been his own.

Pushing a curly tendril of hair from her damp face, Josie sat back on the leafy ground and exhaled. Five tents were now standing, albeit somewhat cockeyed, and Cruz seemed to have the last one under control. Leaning against a pine tree, Josie covertly watched Cruz supervise the final tent-pitching operation. The procedure went rather quickly this time, with no broken pegs or snapped guy ropes. Practice made perfect and all that.

With the campsite nearly ready, all Josie had to do was survive the next two days. That wouldn't be easy. Her heart hammered at the sight of Cruz, and all the mental scolding in the world wouldn't keep her breath from backing into her lungs when he smiled. Yes, she had it bad.

Although the condition had no cure Josie consoled herself that it probably wasn't terminal. Eventually she'd recover. After all, even a common cold didn't last forever. Maybe if she rested, kept warm and drank plenty of fluids, she'd be able to resist Cruz Erickson's charms until she got her strength back.

Now if only she could make it through the weekend—

"Josie!" Donnie skidded to a stop in front of her. "We got big trouble."

She frowned. "Did we run out of tent pegs?"

"Nah." Donnie's expression was ominous. "We don't have nothin' to cook on."

"Of course we do. Have you forgotten the lovely four-burner propane cook stove that was so recently donated to the troop?"

"Yeah." Donnie continued to look morose.

"'Yeah' what?"

"Yeah, we forgot it," the boy said slowly, using the patient tone children frequently bestow on unenlightened adults. "Musta left it in the gym storeroom, 'cause it sure ain't here."

"*Isn't* here," Josie corrected automatically, then she stood and chewed her lower lip. "Did you search Mr. Erickson's trunk?"

Donnie slid her a disgusted look. "Yeah. Like I said, it ain—isn't here."

Cruz appeared. "Donnie's right," he said cheerfully. "No stove."

Josie looked at Cruz with growing irritation. Lord, he was gorgeous. No one had a right to look that darned good wearing a khaki shirt and a funny red bandanna. She folded her arms and glared at him. "You seem delighted by the prospect of peanut-butter-and-jelly sandwiches for two days."

He flashed a devastating grin. "I have no intention of giving up a bacon-and-egg breakfast. We'll simply have to improvise. After all, the Scout motto is Be Prepared, and besides, pioneers and Native Americans managed to survive without propane."

In spite of her black mood Josie couldn't suppress a chuckle. He was right of course. It was time she stopped sulking like a adolescent and started behaving like a leader.

Turning to the nearest Scout, Josie gave rapid-fire instructions. Boys leapt to work everywhere, gathering rocks and wood. Soon a large fire ring had been built, complete with a crossbar supported by V-shaped branches for hanging pots. Some extra metal tent poles laid across the rocks served as support for pans.

The troop congratulated themselves on a job well-done, then scattered to perform the various camp chores previously assigned.

Cruz turned toward Josie, stuffed his hands in his pockets and rocked back on his heels. "Not a bad start," he said proudly, his gaze raking her with proprietary warmth.

Her skin heated and she felt a strange light-headed sensation. Folding her arms, she stared shyly at the ground. "I believe you're going to make a good Scout, after all, Mr. Erickson."

"You had doubts?"

"One or two." Josie continued to avoid Cruz's powerful gaze. It didn't help much. She felt the impact of his eyes on her as tangibly as if he'd been pelting her with lasers. Inhaling deeply, Josie changed the subject. "There's still the matter of a fire permit."

"It's in my backpack." Apparently noting Josie's surprise, Cruz chuckled. "I picked one up from the Forest Service yesterday. After all, what kind of a camp-out could we have without a bonfire?"

Shaking her head, Josie felt an embarrassed flush creep up her throat. *She* should have thought of the fire permit. Those details had been her responsibility, but at least Cruz wasn't going to dwell on her lapse. For that she was grateful.

Still, it was partially Cruz's fault. If he hadn't walked into her life with those massive shoulders and sensual dark eyes, Josie wouldn't be stumbling around struggling to remember her own name.

"Yes... well." She cleared her throat irritably. "Thanks for taking care of that."

Cruz's eyes warmed and his voice held a sexy double meaning. "I hope your confidence in my ability has been restored."

"Your ability has never been an issue," Josie replied curtly, silently noting that his motives were another matter entirely. Not wanting to provoke an argument, she kept this thought to herself. Nevertheless she wondered exactly what Cruz Erickson wanted from her. Obviously he wanted something. The frightening part was that Josie, too, wanted something... and she was beginning to realize exactly what it was.

She wanted him.

As she mulled over this revelation, excited voices interrupted her thoughts. Several of the boys were gathered around Billy, chattering exuberantly. Exchanging wary glances, Cruz and Josie joined the happy group.

"Wow, it's really tough," whispered Richard.

Tran agreed. "Yeah, man, awesome. Can I hold it?"

"No, you might hurt him," Billy stated flatly, turning away.

Josie peered over Donnie's shoulder, fully aware that Cruz was standing close behind. She tried to ignore the fact that his arm was brushing her back and concentrated on the whispering clump of Scouts. When Cruz bent forward for a better look his chest rested gently against her back and Josie shivered.

She'd never felt so restless, so out of control. Her body and mind were alienated, working at cross-purposes. Logically Josie knew that falling for Cruz would mean heartbreak and eventual loss. But another part of her wanted to fling caution to the clouds and spend eternity floating in his arms.

Eternity? Where did that trite romantic nonsense come from? What in the world was wrong with her, anyway? Maybe she really *should* see a doctor.

Enthusiastic voices again captured her attention.

"Geez, Billy, where'd you find it?"

"Weren't you scared, dude? I mean, it's totally excellent and all, but it's kinda big."

"Yeah. Like, I woulda freaked if I'd found it."

Curious, Josie dragged her attention back to Billy's mystery guest, then felt every muscle in Cruz's body suddenly stiffen. At the same moment she saw the colorful living rope dangling from Billy's arm. Josie laughed, both surprised and delighted by Billy's prize.

Cruz was not as supportive. His voice was unexpectedly harsh and shook slightly. "Put that thing down," he commanded.

Billy looked crushed. "Aw, he can't hurt anyone, Dad. He's just a king snake."

"I said get rid of it—*now.*"

Cruz had taken several steps backward and Josie watched in shock as his handsome tan faded before her eyes. Stunned, Josie looked from Cruz to Billy. She saw the boy's chin quiver as he tried to face off with his father. Billy's glasses had slipped down his nose, so the effect was less than intimidating. The snake slithered curiously up the boy's arm and a quick glance at Cruz confirmed Josie's suspicions. The man looked positively ill. Obviously Cruz Erickson was not infallible. It didn't take a behavioral psychologist to see that he loathed snakes.

Billy tried another tactic. "He's just what I need for my science project. I could get an A with a live exhibit, and I really need a good grade, because of that test last week and everything. Please, Dad." His face scrunched pitifully. "Please let me keep him."

Josie touched Cruz's arm in a comforting gesture. "The snake *is* harmless, Cruz. Billy is in no danger."

Cruz shook her off. He was fighting for control, struggling to stand his ground. Josie suspected that if his fine thread of self-discipline snapped, Cruz would throw himself protectively at Billy and tear the poor snake into scaly shreds. Her heart went out to both of the Erickson men—Cruz, who was standing up to something that obviously terrified him, and Billy, who seemed to have a desperate need to win this particular battle.

Josie tried to mediate. "What if Billy promises to put the snake in a box and not take it out for the rest of the weekend? When we get back to town, I'll be glad to let him keep it at my place—"

"No," Cruz said firmly.

Tears formed in Billy's eyes and several of the surrounding Scouts reproachfully shook their heads. Cruz rubbed his neck, then extended a pleading hand toward his son. "I know how disappointed you are. I'm not doing this just to be cruel—"

"Yes, you are!" Billy shouted, surprising everyone with his vehemence. "You don't want me to have any fun."

"That's not true, son." Cruz looked shattered and Josie felt a lump form in her throat. "If it means this much to you to have live exhibits for your science project, we'll work something out."

"I want him." Billy sniffed, then held the snake up and stared into its glossy black eyes. A thready tongue flickered and Cruz flinched.

"He's...much too large to be happy in a box," Cruz said quietly. "Perhaps we can find something, uh, more appropriate."

Josie wrung her hands and wondered why an argument between a father and son would cause her such agitation. All she knew was that she hated this confrontation, hated seeing two people she cared about so unhappy. Words came out in a rush as she tried to soothe and heal the rift between them.

"Your father could be right, Billy," she said. "Why, that snake must be nearly five feet long. He'd be cramped in a box and I'm sure he'd miss all his friends and his forest home."

Billy gave her a withering look.

As the boy stroked the snake affectionately, a palpable silence fell over the group. The troop watched tensely, as though awaiting the outcome of this unexpected but interesting battle of wills.

Finally Billy looked at his father. There was a gleam in the boy's eye that Josie couldn't quite identify. "I'll put him back where I found him," Billy said slowly, then turned and walked away, cradling the snake as though it were a small furry animal.

Cruz exhaled slowly and in his eyes Josie saw no triumph, only sadness and resignation.

The forest was quiet this time of night. By the time the snake fiasco had been resolved and eight young Scouts had been tucked into their tents, the moon had risen high in the mountain sky. With a flashlight, Josie picked her way through the thick foliage to a nearby creek. She settled on a boulder and enjoyed the soothing sound of water trickling over the stony creek bed. That such pristine beauty existed less than a hundred miles from the sprawling L.A. metropolis was amazing.

Josie had personally chosen this spot for the camp-out. She'd found it last year during one of her frequent weekend motorcycle jaunts. She always loved riding through the mountains, enjoying the pine-scented wind and the thrill of piloting fearlessly around hairpin curves and narrow roads. These forays into the unspoiled wilderness refreshed her and cleared her mind.

At the moment Josie's mind could certainly use some clearing.

A snapping branch made her jump.

Turning, she flipped on her flashlight and pointed its beam into the black forest. Dry leaves crunched rhythmically, then she heard the rustle of a disturbed tree bough. Were there bears in this part of the San Bernardino Mountains? Yes, there were. There were also cougars and badgers and coyotes and—

A huge dark figure emerged from the trees. With a gasp, Josie aimed the flashlight as though it were a gun. The beam landed on the moving silhouette and Josie's hand flew to her throat.

"Cruz," she whispered. Relief instantly turned to anger. "What are you doing sneaking up on me like that?"

Cruz sat beside her. "I didn't mean to frighten you."

"You didn't," she snapped irritably, silently admitting that he'd nearly scared her socks off. "I'm just not in the mood for company, that's all."

"Oh." Folding his legs, Cruz propped his chin on his knees and stared at the moonlight bouncing off the narrow stream of rushing water. "I don't like you wandering through the woods at night."

Josie stared at him as though he'd lost his mind. "Next time I'll be sure to raise my little hand to ask permission."

"Fair enough," Cruz said pleasantly.

Josie made an undefinable sound and firmly scooted to the far end of the boulder. She could simply leave, of course, but that's exactly what he wanted. Besides, she'd been there first. She glared into the blackness.

They sat silently for a few moments, then Cruz spoke. "I didn't handle the snake issue very well, did I?"

Josie's irritation melted. "You did what you thought best."

Tossing a small pebble into the creek, Cruz said matter-of-factly, "I'm not too fond of reptiles."

"Really? I never would have guessed."

The moonlight illuminated Cruz's embarrassed smile. He shrugged. "I'm not all that hopeless. I love dogs and cats and small children. I even like hamsters. It's just that my brother had a pet snake. The damned thing slithered into my bed one night and scared the living daylights out of me. My parents spent three hours coaxing me down from the dresser."

The comical image tickled Josie. "That must have been a shock to your system."

"You could say that," Cruz mused, looking across the creek into the darkness beyond. "I was only five at the time. For years I couldn't even look at a snake on television without getting physically ill." He turned and looked at Josie with a serious expression. "When I saw Billy with that...thing, I had this horrifying image of it wrapped around my son's neck, squeezing the life out of him."

"Under the circumstances I can understand why you felt overprotective."

"Overprotective?" Shadows veiled Cruz's face as she glanced away. "I don't believe protectiveness can ever be overdone, particularly with people you love."

"How can you expect children to survive on their own if you keep them in a sterile bubble and don't allow them to make their own mistakes?"

Even in the darkness Josie saw the tightening of Cruz's jaw. His voice was unexpectedly harsh. "Mistakes can be fatal."

Something in his voice urged caution. Carefully she changed the subject. "I didn't realize that you had a brother. I've never heard you or Billy talk about him."

After a long moment Cruz said simply, "My brother died twenty-two years ago."

"I'm sorry. You must have been very young at the time."

"I was ten, I think."

"Had you been very close?"

"Very close considering our age difference. Ray was seven years older, so I really looked up to him. I remember thinking him the bravest person in the entire world." Cruz emitted a dry laugh. "Now I realize that he wasn't brave at all. Merely foolish."

"Why do you say that?"

"Because he was a thrill seeker, always doing crazy irresponsible things. The more dangerous something was, the more determined Ray was to prove himself." Cruz looked at Josie, tilting his head and regarding her thoughtfully. Finally he said, "You're a lot like him."

Startled, Josie said, "You think I'm crazy and irresponsible?"

"In some ways."

"Name one," she challenged, annoyed by the accusation.

"That damned motorcycle."

She shook her head in disbelief. "If you know what you're doing, motorcycles are perfectly safe and they're cheap to operate." Her chin jutted out. "Is that what's been bothering you?"

"Yes, it concerns me to see you bellowing around on that hideous machine," he acknowledged. "And I think it's absolutely idiotic for a woman like you to earn a living confronting armed hooligans. With your education, you could do something worthwhile."

"I happen to think that working with children *is* worthwhile," she said through tightly clamped teeth. The fact that she was defending her life-style was just as irritating as the fact that Cruz questioned it. Josie knew she should simply shrug off his opinions as irrelevant, but somehow she couldn't. For reasons she'd yet to fathom, his opinion *did* matter.

When Cruz spoke again, his voice had softened. "I'm worried about you, that's all. I care what happens to you."

Somewhat mollified, Josie sniffed. "That's all very flattering, but it still doesn't give you the right to tell me how to live. I don't need a white knight protecting me from the evils of the world. I can take care of myself."

Frustrated, Cruz slung another pebble into the creek. "No one is alone in the world. Everything we do affects the lives of others, and as far as I'm concerned, your attitude is rather self-indulgent."

Josie stiffened. "I beg your pardon?"

"You may see yourself as some kind of courageous heroine, but all I see is a reckless woman roaring through life as though danger were her personal guide. Do you believe that you have a moral right to kill yourself? What about the people who depend on you. Don't they have rights, too?"

"No one depends on me," Josie said, suddenly shaken by the vehemence in Cruz's voice and the grain of truth in his words. "I won't allow it. I spent too many years living for someone else. I've been depended on to the point of being smothered and I've had it. My dues are paid, Cruz, and my life is none of your business. Get off my case."

Josie tried to stand but Cruz had hold of her wrist. "That's where you're wrong." His eyes snapped with dark fire. "I feel things for you that make it my business."

Stunned, Josie dropped back onto the rock, more because her legs had given out than because of Cruz's grip on her arm. "W-what exactly *do* you feel for me?"

Swallowing, Cruz looked away uncomfortably. "I'm not sure."

"I see." Folding her hands primly in her lap, Josie stared at her knees. "But it gives you the right to dictate how I conduct my life?"

"Yes. No." He speared his fingers through his hair. "Hell, I don't know."

Cruz sighed in frustration. Josie watched him carefully. There was a pattern here, she realized. Although Josie hadn't identified the particulars, it didn't take a genius to see that his brother's death was still affecting Cruz in a very real way. Perhaps by understanding Cruz's relationship with his brother Josie could glean a clue as to what made this man tick.

Cautiously she broached the subject. "What happened to your brother?"

Cruz looked at her, then through her. For a moment she feared he wasn't going to answer. Then he said simply, "An accident."

"What kind of accident?"

Cruz made a wry face. "Automobile, I think. I'm not certain." Seeing Josie's shocked expression, he explained, "I was very young and, quite frankly, my memory is rather vague."

"But over the years, have you and your parents never discussed it?"

"No. We talk about Ray quite a bit, but I don't recall ever discussing the accident itself. My parents were both devastated and I didn't want to open old wounds."

How sad, Josie thought. A family torn apart by tragedy and compounded by the inability to share their grief. After all the years, Cruz was still dealing with the loss. That he was willing to talk about it now, with her, was a good sign. She encouraged him. "Tell me more about Ray."

Cruz smiled. "He was obstinate and brilliant, confident and fearless. My father was so proud of him. He'd planned Ray's entire lfe, expecting him to follow in his own footsteps."

Josie was getting the gist. "But Ray had other ideas, right?"

"Right. There was constant friction and my mother was always flitting between them trying to patch things up. I was too young to realize that adolescent rebellion was a relatively normal occurrence. I thought Ray was incredibly courageous and I wanted to be just like him." Cruz chuckled, apparently amused by some remembered incident. "The one time I tried to emulate Ray's bravado, my father plucked me off the ground and shook me like a wet rag. Of course my brother was seventeen and topped six feet, while I was just a skinny ten-year-old, a fact I hadn't taken into consideration at the time."

Smiling sadly, Josie tried to envision how her own life might have been changed by a sibling. She'd always dreaded the thought of another person for whom responsibility must be assumed, but maybe it wouldn't have been like that at all. Perhaps it would have been like having a confidant with whom to share joy and laughter, sadness and fear. Then, to lose such an intimate friend . . . Well, Josie could only speculate on the depth of such loss.

"You must have missed him terribly," she whispered.

Cruz's voice grew sad and distant. "Yes, but my parents suffered the most. His death broke their hearts. I tried to make it up to them, but . . ." He shrugged, at a loss for words.

"You were a child. How could you expect to make up for your brother's death?"

"I tried to be a good son, that's all. I was determined never to hurt them by irresponsible behavior, as Ray had done."

"And so you've spent your life trying to atone for your brother's mistakes?"

"I wouldn't put it that way," Cruz said quickly. "I simply grew up realizing that we all have certain expectations to fulfill. I did my best to live up to them."

"How?"

"The usual ways, I guess. I stayed out of trouble, got reasonably good grades and went to my father's alma mater."

Josie imagined Cruz as a bewildered child, stoically suppressing grief, trying desperately to atone for sins that were never his own. As her heart went out to the child he'd once been, admiration blossomed for the strong man he'd become. The attitudes and behavior that had seemed so rigid now made more sense.

Josie regarded Cruz thoughtfully. "That's why you expect so much of Billy, isn't it?"

Cruz didn't balk at the thought. "Probably so. I won't allow *him* to self-destruct."

Josie pondered her next statement carefully. She didn't want to alienate Cruz but felt he was receptive to a gentle warning. "Sometimes when young people are faced with overwhelming pressure they lose all sense of themselves and rebel by rejecting their parents' value systems. If you push Billy too hard it's possible he may react in the way you fear most."

"I know." He took a deep breath, exhaling slowly. "I've been thinking about that lately, worrying about whether I'm doing the right thing by my son. I don't want Billy to feel as though he had to challenge the world to assert his individuality, like Ray." Cruz's eyes pierced the darkness when he added, "And like you."

That got Josie's attention. Straightening, she unconsciously laid a hand on her chest. "Me?"

"Yes, you." Cruz stretched out on the rock, propping himself on one elbow. "The first time I met you, I thought you were a rather strange young lady who had landed on her helmet once too often."

"How quaintly put," Josie replied irritably.

Cruz was undaunted. "I thought you were flaky and capricious, but you've changed over the past few weeks."

"*I've* changed?" Josie knotted her arms in front of her chest and fumed inwardly. "From my perspective, sir, *you* are the one who's done some major personality renovations. You were narrow-minded and self-righteous and absolutely the most pompous pain-in-the-rear I'd ever met."

By the time she'd finished the unflattering description, Cruz had bolted into a sitting position. His comical expression reminded her of the bulgy-eyed carnival goldfish.

She smiled sweetly. "But over the past few weeks you've loosened up considerably. It becomes you."

Cruz glared darkly for several moments, then his mouth twitched. "I'd say we both got caught in the old cliché of judging a book by its cover."

Josie laughed. "I'd say you're right."

"How about that? Total agreement and not a basketball in sight." Cruz's expression sobered. "You're a fine woman, Josie McGee. I respect the way you relate to the boys and admire your ability to cut through superficiality. You care deeply about people, but for some reason you seem frightened when others care about you."

Surprised by his insight and uncomfortable to have the conversation turned to herself, Josie squirmed awkwardly and said nothing.

"We aren't so different, you and I," Cruz added quietly.

He was right, she realized. As a boy, Cruz had been overwhelmed by responsibilities far beyond the capacity of his tender years, as she had been. Cruz had reacted to those burdens by rigidly conforming to the expectations of others; Josie had taken an opposite tack, stubbornly rejecting those same expectations. In more ways than she could have imagined, she and Cruz were much alike. The realization was a shock.

So was what happened next.

Lost in thought, Josie hadn't noticed Cruz moving closer until she felt his palm rest against her cheek. Startled, she turned her head and stared straight into his face. He was very close, so close she saw moonlight reflecting in his eyes.

"Why so sad?" he asked in a husky whisper.

"I—I don't know. It just seems as though life isn't fair and it's the young and the innocent who suffer most."

"You suffered, didn't you, Josie?" Cruz brushed his thumb gently over her brow. "You still do."

"No." Josie tried to turn away, but his soft touch immobilized her. She stammered, "I'm happy with my life. I have everything I want, everything I need."

"Everything?" His question was quiet, yet powerful. "Don't you ever get lonely? I do."

"Everyone gets lonely sometimes." Josie hated the emotional quiver in her voice, but her throat was so dry she was grateful to emit any sound at all. "I . . . cope."

"We all 'cope.' I used to think that was enough, but it's not." Cruz cupped her face with one palm and rubbed his other hand over her back. "I've been searching for a long time and never had the foggiest notion of what I was looking for."

Licking her lips, Josie summoned a burst of inner strength and slowly turned away. Her heart was beating against her ribs as though seeking escape. "Have you found it—what you're looking for?"

"Maybe." Cruz laughed softly. "I never thought I'd find anything like you, though."

"Like . . . me?"

"Ummm." His mouth brushed the back of her neck. "I don't know what's wrong with me lately. I can't sleep, food is about as tasty as sawdust and I can't concentrate."

"I, uh, think we've caught the same virus."

"You, too?"

Josie nodded and saw Cruz's eyes crinkle with pleasure. She shrugged. "Is there hope for a cure?"

"I don't know," he whispered against her cheek. "But the treatment is sure going to be fun."

Josie hesitated, then moaned softly, winding her arms around his neck and unconsciously offering her lips.

With a harsh sound deep in his throat, Cruz cradled her head in his palm, kissing her deeply, intimately. He felt Josie's body melt against him, pliable and warm. There was a sweetness to the moment, a tenderness so intense, tears seeped into his eyes. Nothing in Cruz's life had ever felt so right.

As their kisses grew more urgent, more passionate, a fuzzy voice in Cruz's brain reminded him of the camp beyond the trees. With supreme effort he finally released her.

Both were breathing heavily. Josie looked shocked. He saw moisture bead her thick lashes and knew that she, too, had been deeply affected. At that moment, Cruz wanted her more than he'd ever wanted anything in his life. His feelings went beyond more physical craving. This was the woman he wanted to share his life with. Josie McGee was not the woman Cruz had expected to find, but he knew without doubt that she was the woman he'd been waiting for.

The revelation was so unexpected that Cruz yanked his hands away like he'd touched a hot ember. At the sudden movement, Josie blinked. Then, as though horrified, she gasped and fled into the darkness.

Stumbling into her tent, Josie fell across the squishy sleeping bag and tried to catch her breath. Things had gone much too far. Her inability to control these burgeoning emotions was more than annoying; it was frightening.

Of all the men in all the world, why did she have to make a fool out of herself over someone like Cruz Erickson? They were as different as the seasons, with diametrically opposed value systems. To Josie, true love was allowing a bird to soar unfettered and free; to Cruz, love meant the protection of a gilded cage.

She tossed fitfully, drifting in and out of a restless sleep, until the first spray of dawn touched the mountain. A loud whisper filtered into her tent.

"Josie? Are you awake?"

Blinking into the gray pall, Josie saw a thin silhouette peering through the canvas tent flap. "Donnie? What is it?"

With that encouragement Donnie began a garbled rush of words. "Oh, man, I told the little dude not to go, but he said he'd be right back, then he never showed up and I didn't know what to do—"

Josie interrupted Donnie's frantic babbling. "Slow down. Now, who did what and when?"

Donnie took a ragged breath, nearly choking. "I-it's Billy. He's g-gone."

Chapter Seven

"What do you mean, *Billy's gone*?" Scrambling to her knees, Josie snagged Donnie's arm and hauled him inside. "Where on earth would he be at this hour?" she whispered urgently. "Tell me what happened?"

Gulping, Donnie shook his head. "I dunno. I woke up about an hour ago before it got light and Billy was putting on his knapsack."

Josie released Donnie's arm and sat back on her heels. Knapsack? Why would he need a knapsack to answer a call of nature? "Did you ask him what he was doing?"

"Sure, but he just said he had to find something." Donnie's face twisted. "Man, I thought he was going to take a—well, you know. But he never came back and I didn't know what to do."

"You did the right thing by telling me." Josie comforted Donnie, giving him an assurance she didn't really feel. "I'm certain everything's just fine. He probably went for a little hike and lost track of time."

"But you told us we couldn't leave camp without permission."

Josie chewed her lower lip nervously. "Perhaps he forgot."

Donnie's eyes narrowed skeptically. He obviously didn't believe that for one minute and neither did Josie.

Ignoring the sinkhole forming in her stomach, Josie played the situation through her mind and made a decision. She turned to Donnie. "Go pack your knapsack, then get Richard. Bring him back here, but don't wake anyone else up."

With a brisk nod, Donnie scrambled out of the tent and Josie turned her attention to her own knapsack. She inventoried its contents: rope, knife, canteen of water—first-aid supplies. Satisfied, she slipped her arms through the straps and quietly exited the tent.

The camp was quiet, and for that, Josie was grateful. Cruz would be panic-stricken to know Billy was wandering alone in the wilderness. If she could only get the boy back before his father discovered he was missing, Cruz would be spared some agonizing moments.

Donnie towed a perplexed Scout from a nearby tent. Josie leaned over, speaking in a hushed voice. "Richard, Donnie and I are going to look for Billy."

Richard's eyes rounded. "Where'd he go?"

"Shhh." Josie slanted a glance around the camp. "He probably went for a walk. If Mr. Erickson wakes up before we return, tell him we'll be back in a few minutes, okay?"

"Okay," Richard replied.

Josie motioned for Donnie to follow, then they furtively headed toward the woods.

There were only two exits from the camping area: the dirt road they'd driven up on and a hiking trail into the woods. Given the fact that Billy had taken a knapsack and hiking gear, Josie chose the trail.

For nearly half a mile the duo quietly picked their way over the rocky path, searching for clues. When the rocks dwindled to packed earth, they finally spotted footprints.

Josie's relief was short-lived. The trail headed into a steep wild canyon and her heart leapt. If Billy had gone into that treacherous terrain he could be in serious trouble.

And that was exactly where the footprints were heading.

Cruz's eyelids flew open as though spring-loaded. Branches swayed over the small tent, creating an eerie shadow show through the thin nylon walls. For a groggy moment, Cruz didn't quite remember where he was, then everything rushed back in a vivid flood of memories. They were in the mountains. He remembered last night by the creek, how soft Josie's lips had felt against his mouth, how sweet she had tasted. Cruz remembered the glimmer of tears on her cheeks. The bewilderment in her eyes before she'd turned and run away from him . . . and from herself.

Sitting up, he rubbed his stiff neck, turning his head to loosen the knotted muscles. Lord, he was too old for this. What in the world had gotten into him? Six months ago, he'd have laughed in the face of anyone suggesting that he sleep on a pile of rocks and freeze his buns in the bargain. But here he was and the truly strange part was that the entire experience was actually fun.

Perhaps the lovely sorrel-haired occupant of a neighboring tent had something to do with his mellow mood, Cruz mused. If that delicious dream he'd had last night was a premonition, life was going to be a lot more interesting in the days to come.

A yawn overtook him. Coffee. Even in the wilderness, a man had to have his coffee.

In spite of the cramped quarters, Cruz managed to change into a clean shirt and locate one of his shoes. He'd about given up on the other one until he sat on an oddly shaped lump. By the time he crawled out of the tiny tent, he was in dire need of caffeine.

The sun had risen above the peaks, shining with springtime brightness. Squinting, Cruz saw three Scouts huddled solemnly around a cold fire pit. He frowned. No fire? That was strange. He would have bet that Josie was the type to rise at dawn and stoke a magnificent blaze from twigs and pine needles.

Then he smiled to himself. She'd overslept. This was his opportunity to show off his own survival techniques. By the time Josie dragged her sleepy little body out of the tent, Cruz would have bacon sputtering and coffee bubbling and all manner of delectable scents wafting through the forest. She would, of course, be ever so grateful.

Rubbing his hands together, Cruz strode toward the sober group. "Up and at 'em, guys! We've got a three-course meal to prepare. Who's got firewood duty this morning?"

"Donnie." Richard looked up morosely. "But he's not here."

Cruz frowned. "Where is he?"

Richard shrugged and used a twig to stir the lumpy gray ashes. "He went with Josie."

"Oh. Well, where is Josie?"

"I dunno."

Swallowing annoyance, Cruz spoke slowly, enunciating each word. "If you don't know where Josie is, how do you know that Donnie is with her?"

Richard looked miserable. "They followed the trail."

Cruz scratched his head in confusion. "When?"

"'Bout a half hour ago."

"Why?" None of this made any sense to Cruz, but a peculiar uneasiness tightened his belly. "Why would Josie and Donnie go hiking at dawn?"

"T-they're looking for Billy."

Uneasiness hardened into icy fear. Richard's next words struck like a hatchet blow.

"Billy's gone," Richard said, sniffing. "He ran away."

As Josie had feared, the small sneaker marks led directly into a steep ravine. Left of the path, stands of timber dwindled into a slag rock wall, and to the right, the mountains seemed to disappear altogether, dropping into a sheer-sided canyon.

She paused, trying to swallow mounting panic and get her bearings. A covert glance at Donnie confirmed that he, too, was less than comfortable with the situation. His eyes looked like blue-yoked eggs.

"The trail's g-gettin' smaller," Donnie announced nervously.

Josie had certainly noticed, but managed a limp smile. "I'm sure Billy's just around the bend," she replied with feigned confidence.

"Right," the boy mumbled, skimming a glance over the ledge. "If he ain't down there."

Josie whirled angrily. "That's enough of that kind of talk," she snapped, then instantly regretted her harsh tone. Hearing her worst fear spoken aloud had been nearly more than she could handle; still, falling to pieces wasn't going to help the situation one bit. Closing her eyes, she took a deep breath and drew on hidden strength. When she spoke again, her voice was quiet yet firm. "I'm sorry Donnie. I know you're worried and so am I."

Staring at the ground, Donnie shuffled awkwardly for a moment, then looked up. "I ain't worried...just don't wanna miss breakfast, that's all."

Nodding, Josie ruffled the boy's hair. She knew Donnie was trying to lighten things up for her sake, and appreciated his effort.

For the next fifteen minutes, they carefully picked their way along the narrow path. When they edged around a particularly treacherous section, both were relieved to see the trail expand into a plateau wide enoguh to pitch tents on. Ribbed footprints dotted the terrain and Josie dropped her knapsack, kneeling to examine them. The prints didn't seem to leave the flat area.

Squinting upward, Josie searched the slope above them.

"Hey man!" Donnie's voice startled her. Standing quickly, she saw the boy crouched on a rocky ledge, staring down into the ravine. "How'd you get yourself down there?"

In three giant steps Josie was beside Donnie. There, about thirty feet below, sat Billy, clinging to his knapsack, looking humiliated and scared. Josie's relief turned quickly into concern. The ledge on which she and Donnie stood veered out over the cliff. Billy was perched on a second rocky outcrop, but between the two areas the earth had been weathered away as though scooped out by a giant spoon. The only way up was to climb thin air.

This was not good.

"Are you all right?" Josie called.

"I twisted my knee," came the pitiful reply. "And my head hurts." A patch of crimson stained Billy's hair.

Josie saw the blood and felt ill. Still, she was grateful that Billy didn't appear to be badly hurt. "How did you get down there?" she asked, hoping he'd found a hidden pathway. No such luck.

He pointed to the boulder on which she and Donnie stood. "I slipped off that rock."

So much for secret passageways. Josie sat on her heels and willed her hands to stop trembling. That he'd landed on the small outcropping was nothing less than a miracle. A few inches one way or the other and Billy would have plummeted to certain death.

"Hold on, dude, we'll getcha up," Donnie yelled, leaning precariously over the edge.

Gasping, Josie snagged Donnie's belt and hauled him backward. "Don't *do* that!"

"Sorry," the boy mumbled, then nodded toward Billy. "But how're we gonna get him outta there?"

Josie rubbed her head. "We don't have a lot of options. Get the rope out of my backpack and let's see if it's long enough to reach him."

While Donnie retrieved the rope, Josie searched for something to tie it to. The only object sturdy enough was a nearby tree, but it was several feet from the edge. Still, using a boulder was too risky. The surface was irregular and Billy's weight could cause the rope to slip off. The tree seemed her only choice.

When Donnie handed Josie the coil of nylon rope, she secured one end to the tree trunk. Carefully unwinding the remainder, she checked the entire length for fraying or other damage before tossing it over the edge. The rope danced in mid-air, then dropped to the rocks below.

Well, nearly to the rocks. Peering over the edge, Josie saw that the end of the rope barely reached Billy's thighs. She felt ill.

"Can you tie it around your waist?" she asked hopefully.

Slipping one arm through his knapsack, Bill struggled to tie the end. The weight of the pack dangling from one shoulder caused the boy to lose his balance and he lurched back a step before righting himself.

Josie nearly bolted over the edge in panic. "Drop the pack!" she screamed. "It's too heavy—get rid of it."

Billy rejected the thought with a firm head shake, then again fumbled with the end of the rope. It was obviously too short. The boy squinted up and poked his glasses into place. "I can climb up." He grabbed the rope as though to prove the point.

"No!" Josie shouted hoarsely. "Stay put!"

The mental picture of Billy shinnying up a rope with nothing between him and a thousand feet of air except the strength of his own small hands was terrifying. This situation required immediate assistance.

Turning to Donnie, Josie tried to sound calm. "Go back to camp and get Mr. Erickson. Tell him Billy is all right, but that we need more rope."

Without argument, Donnie whirled and headed back toward the narrow path, skidding to a stop as Josie called out. He turned expectantly.

"Be careful," she whispered, fighting a sudden rush of tears.

Donnie's expression melted. "I will," he promised, then disappeared around the bluff.

Returning her attention to Billy, Josie mustered her most reassuring voice. "Help is on the way," she called cheerfully. "You'll be eating pancakes before you know it."

"Yeah," Billy replied, looking totally dejected. He cradled the knapsack protectively in his arms. A small shower of pebbles rained down and the boy winced as one bounced sharply off his forehead. Then Josie heard an ominous clattering from below the rock on which she stood. She froze, staring down at Billy in absolute horror as the first stone hurled past, missing him by inches.

Oh, God. The cliff was disintegrating. Billy would be killed.

There wasn't time to wait for Cruz; there wasn't time to wait for anything. Without a second thought, Josie grabbed the rope and levered herself over the edge.

Sharp fibers bit into her palms. Her shoulder throbbed, rebelling against the bruising weight as she dangled in space. Then she lowered herself painfully down to the tiny ledge on which Billy stood wide-eyed and terrified. When her feet touched rock she exhaled shakily.

"T-the rocks are going to squash us," Billy stammered wildly, clutching the lumpy knapsack as though trying to protect the stupid thing.

"Nobody is going to get squashed," Josie said firmly although not convincingly. "I'm going to boost you up far enough to get the rope tied around your waist, then you're going to climb up like a little monkey, okay?"

"O-okay." Billy gulped and slid both arms through the straps of his pack.

"Forget the knapsack."

"No."

Josie was exasperated. "You can't shinny up a rope with that thing on your back."

Billy's chin jutted out. "Yes, I can."

"Billy, for heaven's sake—"

"I'm not going to—"

A granite fragment suddenly dislodged and hurtled toward them. Josie threw herself against Billy, pinning him against the cliff as the rock crashed behind them, then somersaulted into the canyon. Peering over her shoulder, Josie watched part of their ledge break away and plummet downward.

There was no time to waste arguing about backpacks. Turning, she made a cradle of her hands and bent her knees, propping her back against the cliff. "Ready?" He nodded, used her hands as a step and hoisted himself up. Josie grunted, then used every bit of her strength to lift him even higher. Her voice cracked with strain. "Can you tie it?"

"Almost." Billy struggled with the rope and after a small eternity, he said, "Got it."

Josie's breath slid out through clamped teeth. "All right, now climb hand over hand just like in gym class."

The weight on her hands eased. She heard Billy grunt, then the weight disappeared and she looked anxiously up. "That's good, Billy, only a few more feet."

How was he going to pull himself up and over that jutting boulder? Josie held her fist to her mouth to keep from screaming. Billy reached over the huge rock, feeling for the rope. All Josie could see were two denim-clad legs kicking air.

Then the legs bent, pushed and disappeared. Billy was safe.

Josie's knees buckled in relief and she slithered to the ground, clasping her hands under her chin. Tears rushed over her face as she offered a silent thankful prayer.

But the nightmare wasn't quite over. The rope was still too short, the ledge was still disintegrating and it was still one hell of a long way down.

And Josie was trapped.

Cruz grimly picked his way along the narrowing path, repressing an urge to break into a screaming sprint. His mind replayed the image of his beloved son, clinging to a rocky ledge, terrified and hurt. If anything happened to Billy, Cruz wouldn't be able to stand it. The thought made him ill. He walked faster, oblivious to his own immediate danger until he heard Richard's frightened warning. "Watch out!"

Blinking, Cruz glanced down and saw his own foot hanging over the edge. Carefully he stepped back onto the path and rubbed his head. He had to stay calm. Donnie and Richard were right behind him and he couldn't allow his own carelessness to put the boys in danger.

Donnie seemed to read Cruz's mind. "Billy's okay," he assured Cruz. "Josie's with him and she ain't gonna let nothing happen."

Cruz managed a smile. "*Isn't*," he corrected. "And you're right. Everything will be fine."

Both boys agreed with forced enthusiasm and the small group continued on. After a few minutes, Cruz noticed that the trail took a sharp bend and from his perspective seemed to disappear. His stomach knotted painfully.

Edging around the curve, Cruz saw a wide flat area. A bright blue knapsack lay on a large boulder and beside it a familiar figure was crouched, peering over the edge of the cliff.

The breath caught in Cruz's throat, then escaped raggedly. With a choked cry Cruz ran across the plateau.

Glasses askew, Billy looked up, then flew into his father's arms, sobbing. "I—I'm sorry," the boy stammered between hiccups, then pointed toward the cliff. "Josie lifted me up... sh-she saved me."

Hugging his son fiercely, Cruz struggled for control, knowing that if he gave in to his surging emotions he'd simply collapse on the ground in a quivering heap. His son was safe. Thank God, Billy was all right.

Sniffing, Billy wiped his dirty wet face. "Did you bring more rope?"

Reluctantly Cruz allowed Billy to step away, keeping a protective hand on his son's arm. "Yes, we brought the rope, but there's no need for it now. You're safe."

"Yeah, but—" A sob broke off his words and Billy gestured helplessly toward the cliff.

Concerned, Cruz again felt cold fingers of fear. Except for Billy the clearing had been empty. Cruz's voice was deceptively soft. "Where's Josie?"

Billy hiccupped and broke into tears.

Frantic, Cruz grabbed his son's shoulders. *"Where is she?"*

His worst fears were realized when Billy stammered, "D-down th-there."

Releasing Billy, Cruz rushed toward the large boulder. Below him a mass of coppery curls gleamed in the sun and Cruz groaned.

At the sound Josie's head tilted back. "Hi. Did you bring a longer rope?"

Struck speechless, Cruz simply gawked. The tiny ledge on which Josie was perched was barely wide enough to turn around on, yet she smiled up as though she didn't have a care in the world.

Testing his voice, Cruz croaked, "What in the world are you doing down there?"

Josie stared up in disbelief. "Counting eagle eggs," came the disgusted reply. "Would it be convenient for you to throw me that rope now?"

The request shook Cruz from his stupor. "I'm coming down," he announced roughly.

"Are you crazy?" Josie's voice raised one octave on each word.

"I'm not going to pull you up like some flopping fish on the end of a line." The thought caused him to break out in a cold sweat. "I'm coming to get you."

"Cruz, wait." The edge of panic in her voice made him pause. Peering over, he saw the color had drained from her face. "I don't want to alarm you, but this little shelf I'm standing on was twice this wide half an hour ago. It will never support both of us."

Confused at first, Cruz focused on the ledge just as a small fragment crumbled and disappeared into the canyon. His heart climbed into his throat.

Josie forced a casual tone, edged by tension. "So how about that rope?"

The rope. Cruz stood shakily, feeling as though he was trapped in some kind of surrealistic nightmare. Automatically Cruz barked orders and Scouts scattered. Moments later, the same stoic tree supported a second rope.

Josie tied herself securely. Wrapping the slack around his own waist, Cruz dug in. "Just hang on, honey," he called. "We'll pull you up." With that, Donnie and Billy grabbed the rope and all three began to pull.

Richard posted himself on the boulder, relaying the rescue progress. "She's off the ground," he shouted. A few moments later, he added, "Five feet to go...I can almost touch her."

Cruz looked up and saw Richard reaching over the edge. "Stay back!" he yelled, startling Donnie and Billy, who simultaneously let go of the rope.

The unexpected release yanked Cruz forward and he lost his footing. As he fell he heard Josie's muffled scream. The rope was shooting toward the cliff like a sprinting snake. Cruz grabbed it, ignoring the pain of stiff fibers tearing his palms. Dirt sprayed as his heels gouged earth; still, he slid closer and closer to the precipice.

From behind, Cruz heard Billy cry out, then there was a din of anxious shouts. The yawning mouth of the canyon grew closer. If he didn't let go of the rope, Cruz knew he'd plunge over the edge.

But if he did let go, Josie would die.

Cruz held on.

Suddenly he grunted under the force of a sudden stop. One foot dangled over the cliff and he felt small hands pulling him backward.

Confused, Cruz blinked, trying to clear his head. Slowly he realized that the three boys were tugging at his arms, dragging him away from the precipice. The rope stretched from the tree like a tight wire.

Josie!

Instantly Cruz yanked away from the imploring young hands. Desperately he crawled to the edge and looked over. He was terrified and nothing could have prepared him for the horrible sight.

Fifty feet below the crumbling ledge, Josie dangled at the end of the rope like a limp rag doll. For a moment Cruz thought she was dead. Then he saw her twist, trying to pull herself upright. He was weak with relief.

Ignoring his bloodied palms, Cruz stood and grabbed the rope, pulling with more strength than he would have believed possible. The next minutes were a blur, but when he saw Josie's hands slide over the rock, it was the most beautiful sight he'd ever known. Assisted by the boys, Josie dragged herself painfully onto the boulder. Only when she was in the center of the plateau did Cruz release his death grip on the rope.

Josie took two steps, then her knees gave out. Breathing heavily, she shoved sweat-damp hair from her eyes, then saw Cruz. He was pale and as stiff as a tent pole. Slowly he stretched out his hand and she saw blood. A tiny whimper escaped from deep in her throat. He was hurt. Cruz was hurt.

Pushing herself upright, Josie stumbled to him. He met her halfway, gathering her in his arms and nearly crushing her against him. She felt him shudder, heard him whisper her name with the reverence of a prayer.

Cupping her face, Cruz covered Josie with kisses as he repeatedly murmured her name. She lifted his hands from her face, gently turning them to display his torn palms. She gasped, choking back a cry of dismay. Tears oozed down her cheeks.

"Hey, none of that," Cruz whispered shakily. "You and Billy are both safe now—that's all that matters."

"But your poor hands—"

"Shhh." Cruz wiped away her tears. "It's just a little rope burn."

Looking up, Josie met Cruz's gaze. "You risked your life for me. If anything had happened to you . . ."

Words simply couldn't express the horror of that thought.

"I'm all right," Cruz whispered. "Everything is fine now."

Was it? Josie wondered. She was still terrified, not by her harrowing experience, but by the sudden realization that she was hopelessly in love.

Back at camp a sober troop of Scouts watched from a discreet distance as Cruz confronted his remorseful son. It was time to pay the proverbial piper. Billy was in deep trouble, and judging from the contrite expression on the boy's face, he was well aware of that.

At the moment, Josie felt little sympathy. Billy's foolish stunt could have had deadly consequences—and very nearly had.

Having just demanded an explanation, Cruz clenched bandaged hands behind him. When Billy stared at the ground, Cruz's eyes snapped angrily. "Let's have it," he growled. "No more games."

Cautiously Billy peeked up, ignoring the spectacles sliding down his small nose. "I just felt like taking a walk, that's all."

Even Josie didn't buy that flimsy excuse. She could almost hear Cruz's teeth grinding in frustration.

Apparently so did Billy. One look at his father's thunderous expression made the boy rethink his position. He swallowed hard. "I—I was looking for lizards."

"Lizards," Cruz repeated flatly. He stared for a moment, as though trying to absorb this fascinating bit of information, then spoke slowly, repeating Billy's statement to assure he'd heard correctly. "You were looking for lizards."

"Right." Billy shifted uncomfortably, eyes darting as though seeking escape, then words rushed out. "You, uh, said I could have live exhibits so I thought maybe you'd let me have lizards and I knew they came out early in the morning to get warm on rocks and—" Billy gulped air, then finished lamely "—so I went to look for lizards."

Josie rolled her eyes heavenward and turned away. Now she'd heard everything.

Billy's gaze swept from Cruz to Josie. "Don't you believe me?"

Cruz's response was a narrowed stare.

"I can prove it—honest." Spinning, Billy ran to his tent and reached inside to retrieve the blue backpack. He slid a furtive glance over his shoulder, positioned himself to block Cruz's and Josie's view, then appeared to be rooting through the bag. In a moment he extracted a container of some kind, then pushed the knapsack back into his tent.

Billy walked toward Cruz holding what appeared to be a plastic container that had been well-ventilated by a sharp instrument. Through the transluscent material, Josie saw two distinctly agitated shadows.

"Lizards," Billy announced.

Cruz moaned.

Moving closer, Josie tilted her head for a better look, then nodded. The shadows scurried about, making tiny scratching sounds. "How in the world did you catch them?"

Billy shrugged. "When it's real early, they're still kind of cold, so you can sneak up and grab 'em."

"Ah." Straightening, she folded her arms. "And was there by any chance a lizard on that boulder by the cliff?"

Billy's head dropped. Slanting a glance at Cruz, Josie saw the color drain from his face. Small wonder. The image of Billy diving for a stupid reptile, then hurtling into space certainly made *her* queasy.

"I'm sorry," Billy whispered. "I'll never do anything like that again—honest."

"You won't have the chance," Cruz said through clamped teeth.

The possibilities of that statement widened Billy's eyes. "Aw, Dad—I said I was sorry."

"Sorry isn't enough for a stunt like that." Cruz furiously plowed his fingers through his hair. "Don't you realize what the consequences of your thoughtless behavior could have been? You could have been killed and Josie could have been killed trying to save you." Suddenly Cruz reached out and grabbed his son, hugged him fiercely. When he spoke again, his voice shook with emotion. "Promise you'll never do anything like that again."

Billy pressed against his father's broad chest. "I promise," he whispered urgently. "I love you, Dad."

"I..." Cruz's voice cracked. "I love you, too, son."

Cradling Billy in his arms, Cruz looked up and saw Josie watching them with tears in her eyes. He remembered his terror, his gut-wrenching cry when he'd thought her dead.

As Josie's eyes met his a spark passed between them. Their silent communication was more powerful than a scream, more poignant than a whisper.

Cruz saw love in her eyes and his heart twisted.

Chapter Eight

Bye, Tran. See you Wednesday." Billy waved through the car window as the final Scout was delivered safely home.

In the front seat Josie leaned against the headrest and closed her eyes. The weekend was almost over and she had survived. Physically, anyway. Emotionally, well, that was another matter entirely.

Beside her Cruz sighed audibly. "I have considerably more sympathy for the plight of school-bus drivers."

"You should be grateful that Richard's father handled half of the boys," Josie replied. "Otherwise we would have had kids tied to the roof rack."

Shifting into drive, Cruz glanced in the rearview mirror. He did a double take, put his foot on the brake and spoke to Billy. "What are you doing?"

Josie turned toward the back seat.

Billy had been peering into the blue knapsack on his lap. Now the boy hastily closed the opening flap and looked up innocently. "Nothing."

Cruz scowled into the mirror. "That sack isn't going to dematerialize if you let it out of your sight. I don't know why you wouldn't put it in the trunk with the rest of the gear."

Billy held the pack defensively. "I just didn't want my stuff to get lost."

Cruz gave up the argument but continued muttering to himself as he guided the car into the flow of traffic. Again Josie closed her eyes and returned to the solace of her own thoughts.

Nothing made sense anymore. When she was a child, Josie's life had been controlled by and was dependent upon other people. Once grown, Josie had taken control of her own life. She'd learned to rely only on herself and to fulfill her own needs rather than depending on others to do that. Josie had been happy that way. She had scores of friends and a job she loved. Her life was filled with excitement and challenge. She'd felt . . . free.

All that had changed, suddenly and irrevocably. Josie no longer felt free; she felt powerless, a prisoner of her own burgeoning emotions. It frightened her.

Josie had fallen in love with Cruz Erickson. She wanted him. She *needed* him. Oh, God.

If she had to fall in love, why did it have to be with a man who represented everything that had hurt her in the past? Cruz supported the work-and-duty ethic that had once turned Josie into a twelve-year-old senior citizen. He had high moral standards and firmly held strong traditional values.

That all sounded nice enough; still, Josie couldn't forget that she had been bastardized, condemned at birth by God-fearing folks spouting the same traditional values. Josie had grown up suffering the sting of disparagement and superficial judgments.

Cruz, too, was judgmental. He disapproved of her clothes, censured her attitude about life and even berated her choice of pets. Yet she'd fallen in love with him.

Billy's voice broke into Josie's thoughts. "I'm hungry, Dad. Can we stop for an ice-cream cone?"

Cruz slanted a glance at Josie. "Does that sound good to you?"

With a weak smile Josie shook her head. "No, thanks. I'd really like to get home and clean up." Ignoring Billy's disappointed moan, Josie stared quietly out the window.

Her pensive expression tugged at Cruz's heart. She'd been quiet and withdrawn since the ledge incident. At first he'd worried that Josie had been more frightened by the experience than she'd admit. Eventually he'd realized that there was something else bothering her, something deeper.

But then, Cruz had also been bothered lately, and Josie McGee was most definitely the reason. The woman had touched a chord deep within him, igniting a passion and a persistent gnawing ache that he'd never experienced before. When he'd thought he might lose her Cruz had lost control of his coveted emotions. Cruz couldn't consciously define these feelings, but he couldn't ignore them, either.

Still, nothing about Josie fitted into Cruz's neatly organized life. While she ignored social expectations, he was bound to those same expectations. Cruz had responsibilities to a son who depended on him; he had family obligations to fulfill.

Since Catherine's death, Cruz had always postponed thoughts of remarriage. There had been guilty moments over the years, moments when Cruz had realized Billy needed a mother's love. At those times Cruz had felt selfish. He knew he should find a proper traditional wife; he just didn't *want* one. In fact every time a woman had applied for the position Cruz had found excuse after excuse as to why the poor lady didn't measure up.

But Cruz had been clouding the real issue. He could see that now. Something had been missing from his previous relationships, something that social breeding and proper traditional values simply couldn't replace: love.

To Cruz this was a startling revelation. Love had always been a word used to describe the emotion of caring for someone. Cruz loved his son. He loved his parents, he loved his friends and he had loved his wife. They were all very proper applications of the word.

And then there was Josie, and the word suddenly took on a new and disturbing translation. This undefinable emotion had struck without warning. How could it have happened? How could he feel like this about a woman so diametrically opposed to everything he stood for?

A red light flashed ahead and Cruz automatically stopped. Pursing his lips, he covertly glanced at the woman beside him. His pulse leapt. Apparently he had no choice in this matter. He was hooked.

Silently Cruz acknowledged that the situation wasn't exactly hopeless. When he'd first met Josie, Cruz hadn't been able to even consider accepting a woman who was the polar opposite of himself. After all, to do so was tantamount to admitting that the values on which he'd based his life had no credence. But over the weeks, Cruz had noticed something strange happening. He and Josie were arguing less and her philosophical ideals seemed more in sync with his own.

Cruz smiled to himself. No doubt about it. Josie McGee was changing.

The silent drive was nearly over. Josie saw that they were only a few blocks from her house and she was grateful. She needed some private time to sort out her strange feelings. The past three hours had been pure torture.

From the corner of her eye, Josie noticed a blurred movement. Turning for a better look, she gasped as a black-and-yellow snake suddenly shot from the rear of the car, propelling itself mere inches from Cruz's ear.

Billy wailed. Cruz bellowed.

Tires squealed and Josie stiffened as though glued to the seat.

"Bad snake," Billy scolded. The boy futilely tugged at the writhing tail as the remainder of the animal draped itself over Cruz's shoulder. Cruz gurgled and jammed both feet on the brake. The car lurched like a drunken rabbit. The startled snake flew forward, then quickly wrapped itself around the steering wheel. Its thready tongue flicked wildly in front of Cruz's horrified face.

Cruz stared into the cold black eyes, swore loudly and jerked the steering wheel toward the shoulder of the road. The sharp turning movement propelled the snake around and down until its head ended up in Cruz's lap. At this point, the creature sought safety by burrowing between Cruz's legs.

With a hoarse croak, a wild-eyed Cruz tried desperately to avoid driving up the nearest telephone pole.

Josie emerged from her stunned stupor, saw where the harmless snake was heading and dove into Cruz's lap in a misguided rescue attempt. Grabbing the irritated reptile, she tried to extract the wiggling animal with as much delicacy as the circumstances would allow.

The car jerked to a stop. Josie held on to the snake for dear life. The reptile bucked and twisted. Cruz roared, pushing himself up so quickly his head hit the roof. The movement took Josie by surprise and her head was pressed against the steering wheel. The horn honked wildly.

Josie had a face full of zipper. She was sprawled across the seat, pinned between the steering wheel and a very personal part of Cruz's anatomy.

With a string of frenzied unintelligible oaths, Cruz struggled with the door handle. Billy continued to wail. The horn continued to blast angrily. Josie's nose was pressed more intimately against Cruz and the cornered snake continued to fight for freedom.

Finally the car door fell open, Cruz leapt out and Josie collapsed on top of the coiled reptile. Billy crawled into the front seat, dragging the blue knapsack. The boy moaned, then frantically began stuffing the snake back into the bag. "Boy, Henry, we're in real trouble now."

Dazed, Josie sat up. Henry?

When Billy finished retrieving the wayward serpent, he secured the flap with a double knot, then slid out of the car, holding the pack like a shield.

Cruz strode angrily to the sidewalk, glaring down at the hapless boy. Under the circumstances Josie didn't blame Cruz for being upset. Still, she found herself standing between the two Erickson males.

Clearing her throat, she said brightly, "Well, that was a surprise, wasn't it?"

Cruz folded his arms grimly. Billy stared at the ground.

Frustrated, Josie turned to Billy. "You promised to put the snake back where you found him and Scouts don't break promises."

Billy peeked up. "I didn't break my promise. I found Henry in my knapsack and that's where I put him."

Josie sighed. Children were so darned . . . literal. At least she understood why Billy had carried that stupid pack all weekend as though it were some kind of extra appendage. Then a thought struck her. She eyed the boy skeptically. "So you weren't really looking for lizards Saturday morning, were you?"

"Yes, I was." Billy was vehement. "Just like I said."

Cruz cleared his throat. "Would you care to reconsider that answer?"

Shifting awkwardly, Billy looked extremely uncomfortable. "I *was* looking for lizards." His voice dropped to a whisper. "Henry was hungry."

Josie groaned. That took the cake. Any moment now Cruz was going to explode and his anger would be justified. Billy had deliberately deceived and disobeyed his father, and the consequences had nearly been disastrous.

But the anticipated explosion never came. Instead Josie heard a muffled sound that was suspiciously like a chuckle. Startled, she looked up and saw Cruz was fighting a grin. He lost and burst into laughter. Billy's mouth dropped open. Josie simply stared.

Cruz even startled himself. He should be angry—hell, he should be absolutely furious—but for some peculiar reason, the situation struck him as positively hilarious. Cruz knew that his expression must have been choice. He almost wished he could have seen it himself. And when the damned thing buried itself in his lap... Well, the entire scene had been a real hoot.

Then Cruz noticed that Billy and Josie were staring at him as though he'd suddenly lost his mind. That's when it hit Cruz with the force of a body blow. All this time he'd believed that it was Josie who'd been changing, becoming the woman he'd wanted her to be. Now he realized that wasn't the case at all.

Josie hadn't changed; Cruz had.

Wrapping a fluffy bath towel around her dripping body, Josie nervously ran down the hall and emptied her closet on the bed. Good grief, how had she gotten herself into this mess? She stared at her meager assortment of dresses. The red one made her hair look like burnished copper, but it was more suitable for a business lunch than a formal dinner. Josie tossed the garment aside.

She eyed the silky blue chemise she'd last worn at a friend's wedding. The dress had always been a favorite, but now seemed much too plain for such an auspicious occasion. Basic black? Too drab. And so it went, until every dress in her wardrobe had been summarily discarded and her closet contained nothing slinkier than white-washed denim.

The evening would be a disaster. She had to get out of it. Josie grabbed the telephone, dialing hastily. "Cruz? Listen, about tonight—"

Cruz interrupted cheerfully. "Mother just called. She hasn't been this excited since Billy had a starring role in the school Christmas play."

Josie's stomach twisted. "I—I hope she hasn't gone to any trouble..." The halfhearted words trailed weakly away.

"Trouble?" Cruz chuckled. "Let's just say that she's changed the menu six times and the cook is ready to quit. Mother is really looking forward to meeting you."

Closing her eyes, Josie suppressed a moan. The cook, yet.

"Cruz, I don't think—" Abruptly, she stopped. To beg off at this late date would be unforgivably rude. Even if she had to swallow a gallon of Alka-Seltzer to settle her swirling stomach, Josie was determined to see it through. She was flat-out scared and the unexpected weakness unnerved her.

Concerned, Cruz's voice filtered softly through the line. "Honey? What's wrong?"

"Ummm? Oh, nothing really. I, ah, just wondered what I should wear. I mean, what would be appropriate."

"Wear whatever makes you comfortable."

"Blue jeans make me comfortable."

She heard his soft chuckle. "That's fine with me. This is just dinner with my folks, Josie, not the inaugural ball."

Josie would have felt better if it had been; at least she would have known what was expected of her.

Cruz's voice was suddenly guarded. "You don't want to come, do you?"

Swallowing hard, she whispered, "I cannot tell a lie."

"You have to come. You lost."

"You tripped me," she snapped. "I had the winning basket in my sights—the game was all but won."

"Sorry to disappoint you," Cruz said silkily. "But you fell on your sweet little bottom without any help from me. I hadn't realized what a sore loser you are."

"And I hadn't realized what a desperate man *you* are."

"That's true enough," he whispered. "Especially when it comes to you."

His husky words made Josie's heart hurdle the nearest rib. In the two weeks since the camp-out, Josie and Cruz had spent nearly every evening together. Things had gone too far, too fast, and Josie was beginning to feel that old familiar panic. He'd become too important to her and suddenly Josie found herself imagining a future with Cruz.

And she knew better than that.

Cruz's voice broke into her thoughts. "Hello? Are you there?"

"Ah . . . yes. Now, about tonight . . ."

"What about it?" Wariness again edged his voice. "Out with it, Josie. What's bothering you?"

After a brief pause, she sighed. "I just wondered if I should bring something—flowers or wine, maybe."

"Not a thing. Mother ordered a floral centerpiece in your honor and the wine for each course has already been selected."

Thank heaven Cruz couldn't see the flush she knew was roaring up her cheeks. Wine for each course? Josie had never heard of such a thing—and a floral centerpiece? In her honor, yet?

The evening was doomed. Josie might as well confess her ignorance of proper etiquette right now. Cruz had a right to know that she would in all probability humiliate him with her lack of social breeding.

She took a deep breath. "Cruz, I'm not sure this is such a good idea."

"Why not?" He sounded hurt.

"It's just that . . . I don't want to embarrass you and Billy, that's all."

"Embarrass us?" Cruz gave a relieved laugh. "You could never do that."

"Don't bet on it," she muttered. "I'm liable to stir my coffee with the soup spoon and I'll probably use the finger bowl to make tea and—"

"Who cares *what* spoon you use?" Cruz suddenly laughed. "You and my mother are two of a kind."

"Oh, right," Josie replied dryly. Even Cruz couldn't honestly believe that the matriarch of one of Orange County's most prestigious families would have anything in common with a woman from a dirty trailer in the trashiest section of the Texas coast.

"I'm serious," he replied earnestly. "Mother has been calling me all morning, worrying about what she should wear and what she should say."

"You're joking."

"Nope. Scout's honor."

Josie fiddled with the phone cord, mulling over this revelation. The idea that an upper-crust socialite like Isabel Erickson could suffer an attack of nerves seemed ludicrous. Still, it was no more absurd than a woman who's spent her adult life scoffing tradition suddenly being struck by an overwhelming desire for acceptability.

Life was strange.

Later that night, Josie sat in the expansive dining room and wondered if her stiff smile made her look like a grimacing clown. So far the evening had rivaled Josie's worst nightmare.

The Erickson home was everything Josie had imagined and more. Decorated with gleaming antiques, sparkling crystal and muted tapestry, the rooms seemed more like photograpohs in *Better Homes and Gardens* than living quarters.

The senior Ericksons had also surpassed Josie's vivid imagination. Isabel floated with grace and elegance, while Gunther strode like a battlefield general surveying a conquered land. The man had eyed Josie with suspicion and obvious disapproval.

And no wonder, Josie thought bleakly. The hostess's ivory silk-and-lace gown made Josie's blue chemise look like a thrift-store bargain. Isabel's hair was styled in a sophisticated upswept coiffure that displayed diamond earrings cascading like a glittering waterfall. As usual Josie's hair curled wildly in an untamed, Little Orphan Annie mop.

Josie felt like a frump.

Although she was uptight and uncomfortable, Cruz was completely relaxed. During dinner he laughed often and seemed to be enjoying the entire affair. Even Billy, dressed to the teeth in formal dinner attire, giggled and enthusiastically joined the conversation. Gunther was polite, yet guarded; Isabel was warm and welcoming.

Through it all, Josie feigned enjoyment, smiling stiffly until her cheeks throbbed as though stretched and glued to the bone.

The worst moment was yet to come. Josie was gingerly eyeing a suspicious vegetable when Billy blurted, "Guess what? Josie has her very own motorcycle, and she even knows how to *ride* it!"

Apparently the boy believed that tidbit of news would favorably impress his grandparents. It didn't. Even Isabel's practiced hostess smile faded slightly.

Gunther's thick brows hitched, then furrowed reproachfully. His voice was cool. "Is that so? How . . . unusual."

Josie just smiled miserably.

Billy wasn't finished. "She has a parrot, too, and he even talks. He says the funniest things, like—"

Cruz interrupted smoothly. "More milk, son?" Before Billy could answer, Cruz changed the subject, turning to Josie. "By the way, I'd thought you'd be pleased to know that Henry has moved into his permanent quarters."

Gratefully Josie picked up Cruz's clue. "Where is that?"

Billy answered. "In the garage, but we went out today and bought a real big aquarium for him. He's got a special light to keep him warm and a big rock to hide under and all kinds of neat stuff."

Unable to contain himself, Gunther boomed, "Who the hell—"

Isabel touched her husband's sleeve in a gentle reminder of his language and Gunther's ice-blue eyes melted like a vaporized glacier.

Josie was stunned. Obviously the rigid Gunther Erickson absolutely adored his wife. The realization warmed Josie and suddenly the Erickson general didn't seem quite so forbidding.

Clearing his throat, Gunther rephrased his question. "Who is Henry?" he asked politely.

"Henry the Eighth," Billy replied with renewed enthusiasm. "He's my king snake."

"Ah." Gunther pursed his lips and nodded.

Isabel's dark eyes widened in surprise but she said nothing.

The strained conversation continued for what seemed a small eternity, but eventually Gunther cleared his throat and pushed back his chair. The meal was thankfully over.

Josie was relieved that she hadn't knocked over a wine goblet or dropped an heirloom silver fork on the floor. The linen napkin had only slid off her lap twice, and when an obstinate baby potato had rolled off her plate, everyone had pretended not to notice.

After the group retired to the parlor Gunther snapped his fingers and an aproned woman appeared instantly. "Brandy all around," he commanded, then leaned back, observing the scene.

With a quiet smile Josie accepted the unwanted liquor and balanced the crystal snifter in her palm. She wanted to go home. It wasn't as though the Ericksons hadn't tried to make her feel welcome; they were obviously quite experienced in the role of host and hostess. But Josie felt ill at ease and out of place. She simply didn't belong here.

Suddenly Josie was aware that someone was speaking to her. Embarrassed, she looked up and saw Isabel, who was smiling kindly.

"You do not seem to care for the brandy." Isabel punctuated her soft statement with a graceful gesture. "Perhaps you would prefer coffee?"

"Thank you, that would be lovely."

Smiling warmly, Isabel looked up at her husband. Gunther gazed at his wife as if the sun were rising in her eyes, then touched her hand with such gentleness that a lump lodged in Josie's throat.

What would it be like to be so loved? Josie wondered, awed by Isabel's ability to transform this rigid humorless man into a caring loving husband with no more than a glance.

Turning to Josie, Isabel spoke. "I have a special way of preparing coffee, which I hope you will enjoy. Perhaps you would permit me to show you?"

A way out. Gratefully, Josie took it and was on her feet in a flash. "I'd love to."

The two women excused themselves, and Josie followed Isabel from the elegant parlor through the marble-tiled foyer. A huge curved staircase spiraled upward and beside it stood a narrow harvest table filled with family photographs. Josie hesitated, her eye caught by a familiar smiling face.

"The picture of Cruz and Catherine was taken six years ago at the wedding of my brother," Isabel said softly, touching the silver frame with her fingertip. "They made a handsome couple, did they not?"

"Yes, they did," Josie whispered. "Catherine was a lovely woman."

"She was beautiful, yes, but also on the inside." Isabel laid her hand gently across her chest. "It was a tragedy that one with so much to offer life would have died so young."

Josie wanted to tear her eyes away from the photograph but couldn't. Cruz looked so young, so happy, and Billy was so very small. The woman had an angel's face, with exquisite, expressive eyes and a warm wonderful smile. No one could compete with the memory of such a woman.

Josie felt a soft hand on her arm. As though Isabel had read Josie's thoughts, she said, "Catherine is their past. You are their future."

Stunned, Josie could only stare. In Isabel's brown eyes Josie saw strength and compassion. Overcome with a strange emotional surge, Josie found herself thinking that this was what mothers were all about—supportive, loving, nonjudgmental. If Gunther Erickson had been a cross for his sons to bear, surely Isabel had been their salvation.

Josie couldn't speak.

Isabel touched Josie's cheek in a tender gesture that was as shocking as it was unexpected. Even Josie's own mother had never touched Josie in such a gentle affectionate manner.

"You have been good for Cruz and for Billy," Isabel told her. "Too long, they have been alone. Now that I have met you I can see why you have touched them so deeply. You are a woman of great strength and deep love."

"I..." Helplessly Josie extended her palm. No one had ever said such things to her and she didn't know how to respond.

Isabel was making some very large assumptions about the future. Josie's relationship with Cruz was changing as quickly as color in a kaleidoscope. In Josie's experience, the future of such relationships was limited at best, fleeting at worst.

No, Josie didn't want to discuss the future. Not now and, if history was any clue, she probably never would.

Lost in thought, Josie hadn't noticed that Isabel, too, had become quiet. Looking up, she saw the older woman holding another photograph, a family portrait.

"My oldest son, Ramon," Isabel said quietly.

The picture was of a dark-haired teenager with a dazzling smile, his arm casually draped around a blond youngster who was the spitting image of Billy without glasses.

"Ramon was a handsome young man," Josie murmured.

With a discreet sniff Isabel nodded, grief etched across her lovely face. "He, too, died young."

"I know. I'm so sorry."

When Isabel looked up her eyes were filled with surprise and curiosity. "You know about Ramon?"

"Yes. Cruz told me."

The dark eyes turned away. "And what did he tell you?"

"Only that his brother had died in some kind of accident and that he missed him very much." There was certainly no sense telling the poor woman that Cruz thought his sibling had been reckless and irresponsible.

Isabel nodded slowly and a veil of caution made her expressive eyes unreadable. "That is all that he said?"

"Yes, why?"

With a sad smile Isabel took Josie's arm. "Come. While we prepare the coffee we will talk."

Josie leaned on the balcony rail and surveyed the twinkling valley below. Isabel had insisted that Cruz show off the lovely view, but from the knowing expression in the woman's eyes, Josie suspected that Isabel was delicately allowing them a few private moments.

"The lights are beautiful," she said now. "Like tiny jewels glittering as far as the eye can see."

Cruz stood close beside her. "I've always loved this view. During the day there's nothing more romantic than crowded freeways and reflections off a thousand roofs. But after dark it becomes a magnificent display, a celebration of the night."

The spicy scent of Cruz's after-shave mingled with the sweetness of blooming jasmine. Josie inhaled deeply, closing her eyes. She felt Cruz gently touch her cheek, then brush his fingertips slowly across her throat. She shivered, mustered all her willpower, then turned away.

He didn't press her. "Did you enjoy dinner?"

"Everything was lovely."

"And was the roast beef prepared to your liking?"

"Yes, it was perfect."

Cruz laughed. "Just as I suspected. We could have fed you whale blubber and you wouldn't have noticed," he teased. "Actually the entrée was braised lamb."

Embarrassed, Josie managed a limp shrug. "I guess I was a bit distracted."

Cruz took her hand, caressing her palm with his fingertips. She found his touch reassuring. "Did my parents say anything to upset you? Sometimes my father can be a bit intimidating—"

"No, really." Extracting her hand, Josie folded her arms, shielding her heart. "Your father was... very polite, and I like your mother very much. She's really a remarkable woman."

"Yes, she is." Even in the dim light she could see Cruz's eyes gleam. "Not quite the snobbish onerous folks you expected, are they?"

Josie's face heated. "I shouldn't have jumped to conclusions."

"Probably not," he replied cheerfully. "Especially when judgmental people are at the top of your own pet-peeve list."

There was nothing to say. He was absolutely right and she knew it. Finally she mumbled an apology.

"All is forgiven." Cruz traced her jaw with his thumb. "You've mellowed over the past few weeks."

"Mellowed? How?"

"You're not as rash—or as obstinate."

"I've *never* been obstinate." Josie winced at her own words. "Well, hardly ever. Anyway, I don't want to change. I like who I am."

"I like who you are, too, but I like who you're becoming even more."

Josie interpreted the statement as a backhand compliment, but her voice relayed displeaure. "And just what is it that you think I'm becoming?"

Cruz shrugged and grinned. "A socialite?"

"Oh, Lord. Perish the thought."

"You must admit that you fit right into the life-style."

Josie stared. Was he kidding? Only a fool or a blind man could ignore the fact that she was as out of place in his parents' elegant home as a turkey buzzard was in a nest of swans. The scariest part was that Josie, for one brief moment of insanity, had *wanted* to belong.

She'd been deceiving herself. Somewhere along the way the fine line between truth and illusion blurred perilously. Modern psychology taught that a certain amount of fantasizing might be healthy, but losing touch with reality was downright dangerous and Josie had been skirting too close to the edge.

During the conversation with Isabel, Josie had been startled to realize that Ray's nonconformity and zest for freedom had closely paralleled her own philosophy. Neither Cruz nor his family had ever accepted Ray, and they would never truly accept Josie, either.

It was time for her to accept that sad fact.

Cruz broke the silence, speaking with unexpected wariness. "What did you and Mother talk about in the kitchen? You were gone for quite a while."

"It takes time to make perfect coffee," Josie responded cautiously, concealing her anxiety with a casual tone. "I was learning all of her secrets."

Nodding, Cruz glanced over the glittering valley. He seemed a bit edgy. "What kind of secrets?"

Josie realized that he was unwilling to allow the evasion. "Isabel simply gave me some insight into your family history. We talked about Catherine and . . . Ramon."

"I see." His jaw twitched. "And what did you discover?"

This was something Josie didn't want to discuss. Isabel had shared her own feelings of distress and helplessness at her family's turmoil. To relay this information to Cruz would be violating a confidence.

But the discussion had also given Josie a deeper perspective on what made Cruz Erickson tick. She had learned, for example, that after Ray's death Cruz had changed, become sober and rigid. He'd been at such a vulnerable age, and from what Isabel said, Josie's earlier suspicions had been confirmed. Cruz had indeed spent most of his life compensating for the heartbreak his brother had caused. The final blow for Cruz had been his wife's tragic death and the prospect of raising his son alone.

Apparently Josie's pensive mood disturbed Cruz. "What did you discover?" he repeated urgently.

Looking up, Josie saw a flash of fear in his eyes. She laid a comforting hand on his arm and said simply, "I discovered that you're a fine man."

He relaxed slightly. "Mothers are supposed to say that. The point is, did you believe her?"

"Yes, I did."

His palm caressed her arm, sliding across her skin with the delicacy of a butterfly's fluttering wing. "I'm glad, because I've discovered a few things about you, too."

She shivered as he gently touched her nape. "L-like what?"

His lips brushed her forehead. "Like how you use that tough-as-nails shell to protect the soft vulnerable woman deep inside—and like the way your nose wrinkles when you laugh." When his mouth found her earlobe she shuddered. He nipped gently, then murmured against her cheek. "You tremble when I touch you."

"Yes," she whispered. The world was spinning, the valley lights blurred in a swirling maelstrom of color. Josie was out of control and at that moment she couldn't have cared less, aware only of Cruz's breath tickling her face and his hands stroking her body and his heart beating fast against her chest.

Then his mouth covered hers, possessing her sweetly. Josie melted into his arms. The twinkling valley paled in comparison to the explosion of light in her mind as his lips parted hers, probing and savoring. Josie's heart hammered wildly and she clung to him, wanting this moment to go on forever.

But nothing was forever, and when the kiss ended, Cruz's voice shook. "This is crazy," he whispered raggedly. "When we're apart it's like a piece of me has been torn away. I want to be with you all the time."

Far below, the valley whirled in a glowing vortex. Josie wasn't certain what was up and what was down, but she was certain of one thing: Cruz was kissing her again and she never wanted him to stop.

Then his mouth hovered mere inches from her own trembling lips. He spoke so softly that her foggy brain couldn't translate. With some effort Josie focused her thoughts, concentrating on his quiet words.

"I need you," Cruz whispered. "I don't know what my life would be like without you—I can't even imagine. I never thought I'd ever say this to a woman, but I'm saying it to you—I need you, Josie McGee. I want you with me."

I need you.

Those three words struck terror into Josie's heart, terror that surged up like a black wall. Josie had been *needed* before; Lena had needed her and had shackled Josie to a childhood of fulfilling those needs.

Because Josie had loved Lena she had tried desperately to do just that. But it had never been enough, and when Josie had finally escaped that unhealthy dependence, she'd been determined never again to be so victimized. Avoiding emotional entanglements was a good safeguard; after all, loving someone too much had been deleterious to her mental health.

And now, as Josie pushed Cruz away, she was afraid of her own emotions. She had fallen in love and that presented an agonizing problem. Cruz had been right—Josie *was* changing, subtly trying to please him, subconsciously attempting to become the woman Cruz wanted her to be. The realization was frightening. Soon Josie would be emotionally dependent on a man who, like all the other men in her life, would eventually leave.

Cruz touched her damp cheeks with his thumb. "Tears? Have I hurt you?"

She could only shake her head.

"Then what is it? What's wrong?"

"I—I'm not ready for this, Cruz." Squaring her shoulders, she mustered her courage and faced him. "I won't sleep with you."

Eyes widening in shock, Cruz stared numbly for a moment, then suddenly gave a soft laugh. "Never?" he teased. "Not even if I make an honest woman of you?"

"Pardon me?"

Sobering, Cruz gently cupped her face with his hands. "I'm not going to say that the idea of making love with you hasn't crossed my mind. In fact it's worn a pretty wide path in there, and if you were to tell me right this very minute that you want me as much as I want you, well, we'd both find out if my car really *can* hit zero to sixty in five seconds."

The delicious image made her shudder. Desperately she tried to rein in her own blossoming arousal. If she touched Cruz intimately, if she gave herself to the blind surge of desire, if she allowed that physical and spiritual bonding, Josie knew she'd be forever lost.

"Don't, Cruz." She hated the pleading tone of her voice, the raw emotion it revealed. "Please..."

He held her tightly, ignoring her puny halfhearted struggle. "Shhh. Let me finish." She went limp and he stroked her soft curls. "Yes, I want you, but I want more than a single glorious night of passion. We might have a lifetime of passion, if we give ourselves a chance."

Josie's fuzzy brain tried to interpret. A lifetime? What did he mean? What was he saying?"

Then a single word seared her brain like a hot brand: *marriage*. Cruz was talking about that staid elusive institution that Josie's own mother had alternately scorned and craved.

In sudden panic Josie pushed away. Her mind was lost in the past as she remembered back.

Paul had still been with them. On that long-ago night, he had tucked little Josie into bed, kissing her cheek and ruffling her hair. "Hit the pillow, moptop. Sleep tight and don't let 'em bite."

Josie had giggled, then pulled the covers up to her nose and instantly pretended to sleep as Paul tiptoed out of the room. Josie hadn't gone to sleep though. She'd lain awake, smiling to herself, enjoying the secure sound of Paul's deep voice filtering down the hall.

She'd felt safe. She'd felt loved.

But Lena's shrill voice had broken the peace. "I don't care about being respectable," she'd hollered. "I don't want to get married and I don't give a fat rat's tail about being snubbed by a few old bats at the beauty parlor."

Paul had remained calm. "What about Josie? Don't you care what people say about your own daughter?"

"What do you want from me?" Lena asked tiredly.

"I care about you, Lena, and I couldn't love Josie more if she were my own flesh and blood. But I'm tired of being nothing more than a blank check to pay your liquor bill."

A glass shattered. "Damn you. How dare you say that to me?"

"I can say that because I love you. You're living in an alcoholic fog. You deserve better and so does Josie."

Lena's faint reply shook. "I'm going to quit, I told you. It's just hard, that's all."

"I know that," Paul said softly. "If we were married, I could help you."

"No." Lena paused, then her voice took on a pleading tone. "Haven't things been good between us? Marriage would just mess everything up."

Paul had gotten angry then. It had frightened Josie because she'd never heard him raise his voice.

"Dammit, I want commitment, Lena. I'm not like your other paramours, satisfied with a few laughs and a cheap thrill."

The argument had gone from bad to worse. Josie couldn't remember the details but she remembered how the screaming had finally ended. It had been a night that would haunt her forever.

First had come Paul's ultimatum. "Either we get married and give Josie the life she deserves, or I'm walking out that door right now and I won't be back."

Then came Lena's furious reply. "Then get out, you bastard! We don't need you—we never needed you. *Get out!*"

And sobbing little Josie had leapt from her bed, clinging to Paul's knees and begging Daddy not to leave her.

Afterward Lena had shrugged it off. "Marriage is just a two-buck piece of paper, baby. It doesn't mean a thing."

"But he's gone," Josie had cried. "You made him go away."

"He was getting tired of us, that's all. You know how men are." Lena had held Josie then and said, "I don't need anybody else as long as I've got you, right? You'll always take care of your mama—promise you'll never leave."

Ignoring her own tiny tears, Josie had wiped her mother's damp face and solemnly promised never to leave her. But eventually Josie had broken that promise. She, too, had left Lena.

Cruz's voice brought Josie back to the present. He was watching her with concern. "Josie? Are you all right?"

Her chin raised defiantly. "I'm fine, thank you. It's been a lovely evening, but I'd like to go home now."

Confused, Cruz took a step back. "Josie, I've been talking about our relationship and all you can say is that you want to go home?"

"I'm really quite tired."

He regarded her thoughtfully. "What are you afraid of, Josie?"

"I'm not afraid of anything, Cruz, not one damned thing." She turned on him. "Not every woman in the world swoons at the opportunity of throwing away her freedom."

In horror, Josie looked up and saw the hurt in Cruz's eyes. She could have bitten off her own tongue. In fact she had absolutely no idea where those hateful words had come from; they had simply gushed out of her mouth and she'd had no more hope of controlling them than of switching off the moon.

"Cruz, I didn't mean—"

"You meant every word." Stepping back, Cruz slid his hands into his pockets and considered her. "The question is why?"

"I don't know," she admitted weakly.

Josie was confused. Cruz obviously wasn't going to march angrily away from harsh words as Paul had done. Is that what she had expected? Josie wondered. Had she been trying to drive him away?

Pursing his lips, Cruz contemplated her response, then said, "Running never solved anything, Josie, and it won't erase what we feel for each other."

"I'm not running..." The lie evaporated. Cruz's quiet words had touched a deep long-hidden truth. Josie *had* been running; she had done so in one way or another much of her adult life. But had she been running toward freedom or away from commitment?

To that question, Josie had no answer.

Chapter Nine

Cruz saw Josie avert her gaze, then discreetly blot tears. The gesture touched him. He suppressed an urge to pull her into his arms and kiss away her pain. It took a tremendous toll on his self-discipline, but Cruz realized that he'd pushed too hard. He's seen fear in Josie's eyes like the terror of cornered prey.

Josie, for all her bravado, was afraid. Her expression was fragile, wounded, and for a blind moment, Cruz wanted nothing more than to exact painful revenge on whoever had hurt her so deeply.

The moment passed and, with it, his crazed thirst for vengeance. Josie was all that mattered now and although Cruz ached to hold her he kept his hands stiffly at his side.

He cleared his throat. "I'm sorry. I didn't mean to come on so strong."

"I...ah...probably overreacted." Josie nervously licked her lips and stared into the night.

She looked so lost Cruz had to ball his fists to keep from reaching out. The strain was reflected in his voice. "You simply need time to think things out. Perhaps we both do."

Josie nodded miserably, then whispered, "I'm sorry. It's just that I want—"

Cruz waited, then coaxed gently, "What do you want, honey?"

Then Josie met his gaze with startling intensity. "I want things to be the way they were between us."

Cruz felt his gut tighten. "In what way?"

Shaking her head, she shrugged helplessly. "I . . . want us to be friends."

The simple statement knotted his stomach. Josie might as well have said she loved him like a brother. It would have been just as devastating. Still, Cruz forced a calm expression. "We tried that," he said simply. "It didn't work."

Her eyes shimmered beneath a sheen of tears. Cruz saw a white flash of teeth as she bit her lower lip to still its trembling. "I know," she finally murmured. "What do you want from me?"

"I want you to stop fighting yourself. You're allowed to feel what you feel, want what you want . . ."

"And be what I am?" Her eyes challenged him.

"Yes." Cruz took a deep breath. "I'm simply asking you to give us a chance."

"For how long? Three months? Six? Then we shrug it off and go our separate ways?"

Chin high, expression firm, Josie appeared in complete control. But Cruz saw a frailty in her eyes, a silent plea for him to deny her words. Suddenly he understood. Josie was afraid of abandonment. Her constant battle to maintain emotional distance now made sense to him.

Tenderly, he laid his palm on her cheek and answered her question. "For as long as it takes, for as long as we've got. Maybe forever."

"Can you promise me forever, Cruz?" The tight line of her mouth couldn't hide the hope in her eyes.

"No, I can't." Cruz wanted desperately to give her the promise she sought but he couldn't. It was too soon. "Would you believe me if I did?"

The hope drained away and she shook her head. "Nothing lasts forever."

Cruz gently grasped her shoulders, forcing her to look at him. "Some things do. Love does."

Eyes rounding, she whispered, "Love?"

Releasing her, Cruz spun away and speared frustrated fingers through his hair. Lord, he hadn't meant to say that. "Look, I'm as bewildered by this whole thing as you are. I don't know what I'm feeling. This power you have over my mind and my body just confuses the hell out of me." He faced her. "But we can't go back and I don't believe that's truly what you want. Things have gone too far and what we feel goes too damned deep. We'll go forward at any pace that's comfortable for you—but we *will* go forward. We have no choice."

A torrent of emotion flickered across Josie's face. She touched her forehead as though feeling faint, then squared her shoulders, spun on her heel and started toward the house.

Cruz grabbed her wrist. "Don't run from me, Josie. Please."

The ragged plea jolted Josie inside and out. For the first time she realized that her own turmoil was not so different from what Cruz was feeling. He hadn't lied to her, hadn't tried to exploit or manipulate her with counterfeit promises. Cruz had simply said that he didn't know but was willing to find out.

Was she willing? Josie wondered. Did she have the courage to give them a chance as Cruz had asked? Never before had Josie avoided risks, but the stakes had never seemed so high. An emotional mine field lay ahead, fraught with danger and disastrous potential. Cruz was willing to face these perils; Josie could do no less.

Maybe it *was* time to stop running.

As the doorbell rang Walter clawed air, twisted his feathery neck and squawked, "By the shores of Gitche Gumee...awwrk...shining Big-Sea-Water." He cocked his head hopefully, awaiting praise.

Josie managed to mumble, "Good bird," then called out, "Come on in, Cruz. I'm almost ready."

The front door opened. "What do you mean, *almost*?" Folding his arms, Cruz managed a fake scowl and tapped his foot in feigned impatience. "Five minutes, lady, then we're scrapping this whole idea and heading to the art gallery."

Josie slipped on a worn denim jacket, flipped her beaded dangle earrings over the collar and grinned. "A deal's a deal, mister. You take me to the motocross race today and I'll stroll through a boring hall filled with god-awful paintings next week."

Shrugging his eyebrows, Cruz nodded toward the bedroom door and said silkily. "There *are* other options."

Walter screeched indignantly.

"Not in front of the b-i-r-d," Josie said primly. "Besides, we've already discussed that particular option, so get your libido under control."

Sighing, Cruz took his defeat with relative grace. "It would be considerably easier if you didn't look so damned sexy."

Josie laughed and batted her eyelashes. "Why do you think I wore blue jeans and a flannel shirt? I just knew it would drive you mad with passion."

Before Josie could react Cruz reached out and pulled her into his arms. "And you are right," he whispered, brushing his lips across her throat. "Flannel turns me on." His mouth captured hers with soft urgency and she responded with equal fervor.

It had been two glorious weeks since the Erickson's dinner party, and during that time, Cruz and Josie had seen each other almost every night. True to her word, Josie had stopped running, promising to take each day as it came and simply allow herself to feel what she felt.

And she felt wonderful. She loved Cruz and wasn't afraid to admit it; at least, not to herself. For Josie, that was a tremendous achievement. She trusted Cruz as she'd never trusted anyone in her life. He cared for her; she knew that. Perhaps he even loved her, although he'd never said as much.

Still, they had something special and at moments like these Josie had even convinced herself that forever might come true. Without Cruz her life would be empty, her heart would be empty. She simply couldn't bear to consider the possibility and so she pushed any secret doubts to the deepest darkest corner of her mind

Now she clung to Cruz, returning his intimate kiss stroke for stroke, wanting more of him than she'd ever dreamed possible and knowing without doubt that she wouldn't deny him or herself much longer. She couldn't. Somewhere deep inside, their souls were bonding; soon kisses wouldn't be enough.

Finally Cruz stepped away, took a giant breath and said, "Honey, if we don't leave now, I guarantee we never will."

Shakily Josie cooled her face with her palms. "Right," she mumbled, wondering if she really wanted to see a bunch of racing motorcycles, after all. She was considering a change in plans when Cruz groaned in frustration, then spun and walked quickly to the porch.

"Let's go," he muttered irritably, then headed toward the car.

Josie had little choice except to grab her bag and follow.

Nearly two hours later Cruz stared at the endless barren hills. "We must be halfway to Las Vegas by now."

"Hardly. We're not even to Barstow."

The news didn't cheer him one bit. "Where the hell is this place, anyway?"

"Just a few more miles to the turnoff." Josie patted Cruz's taut thigh. "You'll have a great time."

"I seriously doubt that," he grumbled. The last thing Cruz wanted to do was spend an afternoon watching a bunch of foolhardy daredevils attempt suicide in front of a frenzied bloodthirsty mob and he said so.

Josie sobered. "It's not like that at all. These people simply love to ride. They've put a lot of time and money tuning their bikes into fast efficient machines and they enjoy the competition. It's no different from any other sport."

"That's stretching it a bit."

"I don't think so. Marathon runners train and sweat and tune their bodies for competition, and so do ball players and gymnasts—all athletes do."

"Racing is different. People get killed." Cruz's grip tightened on the wheel. He knew what was coming. Josie was going to point out how people get killed on the freeway, or by falling off ladders in their own backyards. They could debate the subject forever, but the fact remained that the closer they got to that lousy track the colder Cruz felt.

But Josie didn't argue. Instead she surprised him by simply saying, "Racing can be dangerous, I suppose, but the riders are quite skilled and every possible precaution is taken. I've been coming to these events for years and I've only seen one serious injury." There was a pause, then Josie said quietly, "We don't have to go if it upsets you this much."

Now Cruz felt silly. "I promised to take you and I will."

After a few silent moments Josie spoke. Cruz noted a tense edge to her voice. "We don't have to enjoy the same things, but I seem to remember something about respecting each other's differences."

Cruz winced, recognizing his own words. Josie was right. After all the deep gut-wrenching discussions about allowing her to be herself Cruz realized that subconsciously he was still convinced that in some respects Josie would change.

Apparently she was well aware of that expectation. "I won't force you to share parts of my life that make you uncomfortable," she told him firmly. "But I won't be controlled, Cruz."

"I'm sorry. I shouldn't criticize your choice of entertainment, particularly when I don't know anything about it."

"No, you shouldn't." Josie sounded surprised, as though she hadn't expected Cruz to admit that. Still, she was watching him with a strange mixture of sadness and suspicion.

Cruz didn't blame her. What was wrong with him, anyway? It was just a bunch of stupid dirt bikes buzzing around a dinky track. Josie was a sensitive empathetic person. Surely she wouldn't enjoy watching a sport in which participants were routinely maimed. Cruz knew he'd overreacted; he just didn't know why.

He managed what he hoped was a convincing smile. "Actually the entire experience may be rather interesting. I'm . . . looking forward to it." Cruz winced at his last statement and hoped his nose wouldn't start to grow.

But apparently Josie was reassured. She relaxed and laid a hand on his knee. "You might even have a good time in spite of yourself. Oh, turn here."

Grateful for the change in subject, Cruz followed Josie's directions, leaving the highway and traveling a rough gravel road into the distant hills. Half the freeway seemed to be heading into those same hills, much to Cruz's surprise.

As he steered around a wide curve Cruz saw a valley below. Hundreds of cars dotted the landscape beside a geometric dirt track as dust billowed behind like dirty rooster tails.

At this distance the huge crowd looked like color-coded ants, but Cruz could see that the motocross was obviously a major event. The realization came as a shock. Cruz had expected to find a mere handful of riders and had assumed the few onlookers would consist of tattooed biker types garbed in leather and chains.

So much for uneducated assumptions, Cruz thought wryly. Thank heaven he hadn't spouted his pompous conclusions aloud. He felt like a fool but at least Josie didn't know that.

As they drove closer Cruz saw that the crowd consisted mainly of family groups. Children ran everywhere, screaming and laughing. Several rows of motor homes and neatly arranged recreational vehicles reminded Cruz of a suburb on wheels.

Parking attendants controlled traffic, directing Cruz to the end of one neatly organized row. Flipping off the engine, Cruz stared out the windshield, stunned. No, this definitely was *not* what he'd envisioned.

Josie's soft chuckle broke into Cruz's thoughts. "Not quite what you were expecting, ummm?"

Startled, Cruz looked over to see her eyes twinkling with amusement. He shook his head, smiling. "Was it that obvious?"

"When your jaw fell into your lap I had a clue," Josie replied cheerfully. "Are you ready?"

Obviously Josie was more than ready. She'd swung open the passenger door and had one foot out. Her cheeks were flushed with excitement and Cruz laughed, enjoying her pleasure.

"You bet," he said. "Let's do it."

They headed into the throng. Cruz was fascinated by everything, his head swiveling to take in the sights. Finally Cruz grabbed Josie's hand, fearing she'd disappear into the crowd when he stopped to gawk at the shiny powerful machines.

The first hour flew by. Josie led Cruz toward the pit, which was actually no more than a holding area for the bikes and maintenance crews. And Josie seemed to know everyone, introducing Cruz to person after person until names and faces blurred together. When the race started Josie dragged Cruz to the front of the crowd for a better look.

"Josie?" A feminine voice caught their attention as a blond woman pushed through the crowd. "My stars, Josie, I haven't seen you in months."

"Lynda Collins! How on earth have you been!" Josie hugged the woman, then turned to Cruz. "Lynda's husband, Phil, rides for the Borg Oil team. He taught me everything I know about motorcycles."

Before Cruz could do more than murmur a polite acknowledgment the two women were involved in animated conversation. After a moment Lynda said, "We've got a blanket spread by the south curve. Please join us."

"Well..." Josie skimmed a questioning glance at Cruz.

He melted. "Sure. It'll be fun."

They followed Lynda until the crowd thinned, then a small helmeted creature in padded spandex leapt up and waved.

"This is Phil, Jr.," Lynda said, hugging the boy. "We call him Philly."

The helmet turned and Cruz heard a muffled, "Hi." All he could see, however, was his own reflection in the visor's polished surface.

As Lynda pulled out folding chairs Cruz whispered to Josie, "Why is the boy all suited up like that?"

"He's racing in the PeeWee Division."

"PeeWee? You mean a kid like that actually gets on a motorcycle and roars around the track?" Cruz was in shock. The boy couldn't have been more than eight years old.

Lynda handed Cruz a chair and laughed. "Yep, and he's pretty darned good at it, too. He's been riding since he was five."

This was all too much for Cruz. He sat heavily and stared out over the riding area. It wasn't merely an oval track; it was a hodgepodge of hills and jumps and obstacles. Suddenly Cruz was aware that Lynda was still chatting away. He politely turned his attention to her.

"There are several children's divisions," Lynda said cheerfully. "Then they graduate to the Novice Adult classes and finally to the Open Division—that's where the pros race for practice."

Cruz nodded as though it all made sense.

Beaming, Lynda continued, "Each division has several heats—that's so there won't be too many riders on the track at one time. The winners move into the semifinals, then the finals."

"How interesting," Cruz murmured politely.

Lynda's breathless explanation was interrupted by the appearance of a wiry man for whom she seemed to have some affection. At least she kissed him as though she did.

"Hi, Phil," Josie said, standing as she introduced him to Cruz.

Phil flashed a smile and firmly pumped Cruz's hand. Judging by the man's colorful uniform, Cruz judged that Phil, too, was planning a run around the track.

Turning to Josie, Phil emitted a low whistle. "You're looking good, Jo. Racing today?"

"Not today," Josie replied.

Cruz's heart went momentarily silent. Racing? Josie?

Apparently he'd spoken aloud, because Phil was happy to expand. "Josie's one of the best," he said proudly. "She got too damned good for the Novice Division years ago and she's been pushing the pros in Open."

This tidbit of news was somewhat unsettling. Cruz comforted himself with the fact that, judging from her friend's reaction, Josie hadn't raced in quite a while. He really didn't have much time to dwell on the thought because the first heat was beginning.

Soon Cruz was swept up in the excitement, firing technical questions at Josie and rooting for the competitors. At first he'd been a bit tense, particularly when one of the racers took a nasty spill. But the rider had simply leapt to his feet, dusted himself, then hauled the machine up and zoomed back into the race.

Cruz was thoroughly enjoying himself.

Later Josie sat back, feeling more contented than she had in a long time. Philly had returned to the blanket, flushed with excitement because he'd made it into the PeeWee finals and his dad had taken the first heat in the Pro Division. Now the boy was happily explaining racing terms to Cruz, who honestly appeared interested.

A hand on Josie's shoulder startled her. She turned. "Dan! How are you?"

Dan looked tense. "Fine, fine. Uh, listen, Josie, Phil wants to see you in the pits."

Josie was a little surprised, but assumed Phil wanted to show off his new racing machine. She turned to Cruz. "Would you like to come?"

Grinning, Cruz flicked his hand in a careless wave. "You go ahead. Philly is enlightening me on the proper angle to approach a banked curve."

With that, Cruz returned his attention to the animated boy and Josie followed Dan through the crowd.

The pit area was a deafening din of shouted commands and revving engines. They found Phil tuning his bike.

When Phil saw Josie he stood and got right to the point. "Jo, we got a problem. Beecher is scheduled for the next heat and the damn fool just got his foot run over."

"Lord, how did that happen? Is he all right?"

"He was standing too close to the test area and one of the bikes lurched forward. He's okay, but he can't ride." Phil's impatient gesture indicated that the reason was less important than the result. "Fact is, if we have to scratch Beecher's ride, Borg Oil will be disqualified from the team competition."

"Oh." Josie was a bit bewildered as to why Phil was telling her all this. "That's a tough break."

"Yeah, but we still got a shot." Phil favored Josie with another dazzling smile. "All we need is a substitute rider."

Josie got the message. She didn't like it. "No way," she said vehemently. "I haven't raced in six months and I haven't even tested the feel of Beecher's machine. Forget it."

The disappointment on Phil's face hurt. If he'd gotten angry, Josie would have simply walked away. If he'd tried to coax or manipulate, resisting him would have been easy. But he didn't. He simply gave her a sad smile, patted her shoulder and said, "That's okay, Jo. Thanks, anyway."

Phil didn't even remind her that Borg Oil had supported Josie in the past, had in fact been the only team willing to put a woman in the Open Division. But then, he didn't have to. Josie was well aware of how much the team had done for her and how little they'd asked in return.

With a quiet sigh Josie folded her arms and called herself every kind of a sucker. Then she slanted a glance at Phil. "Got a spare helmet?"

Phil grinned.

Pointing toward the next congregation of racers, Philly shouted, "Look! Who's that?"

Cruz looked, but didn't know what he was supposed to see. It appeared to be the start of the third pro heat, with a half dozen helmeted riders lining up their machines. Squinting, he noted the Borg entrant, recognizing an orange-and-blue uniform like the one Phil was wearing.

Curiously Lynda peered toward the group, shading her eyes. "I don't know who that is, Philly. It sure isn't Beecher— Well, I'll be darned."

Cruz followed Lynda's gaze. The Borg team rider was straddling a shiny red machine with fat knobby tires, guiding the bike to the starting line and gunning the engine. Nothing unusual here from what Cruz could see. Still, the rider was slender and strangely familiar.

Then a sparkle caught his eyes as a bauble dangling below the helmet caught the sun. Earrings. Beaded earrings.

Josie's earrings.

Cruz went into shock. *Josie.* It couldn't be.

But Lynda confirmed his worst fear, slapping Cruz on the shoulder and chortling. "This is your lucky day! You're going to see what kind of stuff your lady is made of."

That was exactly what Cruz was afraid of. Oh, God. Josie was on that huge menacing machine—that *red* machine—and Cruz couldn't swallow the sudden rush of fear that flooded him. His mouth went dry, his hands went cold and his lungs tightened into a hard knot.

"Hey!" Lynda's voice sounded a million miles away. "Don't you want to watch the race?"

But Cruz was already pushing through the throng, panting as though he'd run a marathon. He had to get to Josie, get her away from that demonic red motorcycle.

Lunging into the pit area, Cruz sprinted toward the track.

"Hey, man. You can't go out there." A strong hand grabbed Cruz's arm. Without taking his eyes off Josie, Cruz yanked away and careered forward. Something had hold of him again and Cruz struggled desperately.

"Let go," Cruz croaked. "Got to stop her."

Phil's voice tried to soothe him. "She'll be fine, man. Jo's a good rider—"

The words ended abruptly as Cruz took a desperate swing at whatever was holding him back. Phil ducked and swore, then someone came up from behind and wrapped huge beefy arms around Cruz's chest.

"Are you tryin' to kill yourself? You can't go out there..."

Cruz heard excited voices echoing in his brain, but concentrated only on the terror inside of him. *Josie.* He had to get her.

"Hold him, Dan!"

A muttered oath. "The man's gone crazy."

"Get him on the ground— Ouch! Damn! Don't let loose of him."

From the track a roar of accelerating engines bellowed through Cruz's foggy brain. He stiffened and saw the motorcycles tear away from the starting line in a burst of dust and noise.

It was too late. She was gone in a fiery red blur.

Just like Ray.

Suddenly Cruz flashed back. In his mind, he saw darkness and heard engines roar. Then, as though it had happened yesterday, Cruz remembered.

Ray had been sneaking out the back door and Cruz had caught him. "Get lost, squirt," Ray had whispered. "You never saw me, got it?"

"Take me," Cruz had begged. "I won't tell if you take me with you."

"Geez, what the hell am I gonna do with a wimpy ten-year-old? Go to bed and keep your trap shut."

Cruz stood his ground. "I'll tell."

Finally Ray had snapped. "Come on, then, and for God's sake be quiet."

They'd sneaked into the shiny red car and driven off. Cruz had been ecstatic. He'd felt ten feet tall, quite daring and reckless. Even when Ray pulled into the concrete channel of the dry riverbed, Cruz hadn't realized what was happening. He'd only known he was with his big brother and everything was great.

Only it hadn't been so great. There had been a lot of shiny cars in the channel that night, all revving their engines and lurching in challenge. It had been a drag race and Ray was the defending champ.

But Cruz had been disappointed to find that Ray wasn't planning to drive that night. When a rowdy group of kids taunted Ray, Cruz had begged his brother to race and to win.

"Don't let them call you those names," Cruz had pleaded. "Show those goons that you're the best. Show them what you can do."

Finally, Ray had agreed, lining up the shiny red car at the starting line. Cruz had been proud.

Then the teenager had grinned and winked, giving his little brother the thumbs-up signal an instant before stomping the accelerator. The engines bellowed, tires squealed and the acrid odor of burning rubber blanketed the humid air.

Then something had gone wrong.

Brakes shrieked. Glass shattered. The ground shook. Steel twisted like crushed tinfoil as the red car slammed into the embankment. Flames burst from the rubble.

And a horrified ten-year-old watched his brother die.

Now, clinging to the rope fence at the track boundary, Cruz again watched in helpless terror and wondered if Josie, too, would die.

Pulling off her helmet, Josie laughed and shook out her hair. "Whew. What a ride!" She handed the helmet to Phil. "Third place isn't great, but beggars can't be choosers, you know."

Phil simply nodded morosely.

Josie cocked her head. "Look, I know I didn't win, but that's no reason to break into tears. What's going on?"

Phil jerked a thumb over his shoulder. Josie followed his gesture and saw Cruz, standing like an ashen statue. His dark eyes were cold as a cavern and just as menacing.

"Cruz, what on earth—?" His furious expression choked off her question.

Suddenly Cruz strode forward, stopping so close she could feel his breath on her face. He spoke raggedly. "Don't . . . ever . . . do . . . that again."

Josie's eyes narrowed. "Pardon me?"

"You heard me." Cruz's voice could have etched steel. "No more racing. No more metal monsters. Period."

"I see." Josie stepped back as though his words had punched her. She swallowed her mounting anger and ignored her growing confusion. "I don't recall asking for your opinion."

"This is not an opinion," Cruz grated through clamped teeth. "It is a fact. No motorcycles."

Knotting her hands together, Josie met his hard gaze. With some effort she kept her tone calm. "I don't care for edicts, Cruz, and as long as we're on the subject, I don't care for your tone, either. In case you hadn't noticed, I usually do as I please."

"Not anymore. You'll do as I say or—"

"Or what? You'll have me chained in irons? You'll spank me and send me to bed without supper?" Josie lost it and her indignation exploded. "Who the hell do you think you are? What right do you have to give me orders?"

Cruz's skin was the color of dead embers. "I am a man who *cares* about you and that gives me all the rights in the world."

Josie's voice was deadly. "Not quite." Then she spun around and started to leave. Cruz had hold of her wrist before she'd even realized he'd reached out. She stared at the invading hand. "Turn me loose."

"Not until you promise you'll never get on one of those things again."

"I'm not going to promise anything," she snapped. "I'm not a child and I won't be treated like one."

Cruz's voice went up an octave. "Then stop acting like one."

She whirled on him. "You can bully your son but you can't bully me. I do what I want, when I want to do it. You have nothing, I repeat *nothing*, to say about it."

"I have plenty to say about it," Cruz shouted. "I'm not going to stand back and watch you kill yourself for a fast thrill."

"Nobody's dead, for crissake!" Josie yanked her wrist loose and threw up her hands in frustration. What was wrong with Cruz, anyway? He looked like he'd seen a ghost and was acting crazy, as though he'd completely lost control of his mind. Deep down, Josie realized that something was very wrong here, but that realization was overshadowed by the fact that Cruz's behavior was pushing every one of her own secret buttons.

His voice shook. "Let's go. We'll talk about this later."

"No." Her mouth was drier than the surrounding desert. She trembled. "You go ahead. I'll catch a ride with Phil and Lynda."

"I'm not leaving you here."

"Unless you plan to tie me up you have no choice. I'm staying."

For a moment Josie thought Cruz would simply pick her up and throw her over his shoulder. His fists clenched and his jaw twitched tensely. Finally he said, "This is the last time I'm going to ask. Will you come with me or not?"

"No," Josie whispered. "I won't."

With that Cruz stared at her briefly, then whirled away and disappeared into the crowd. Josie felt numb.

For weeks everything between them had been glorious. Too glorious. A pit the size of Wyoming suddenly opened inside her stomach. Secretly Josie had known Cruz seemed too good to be true. Such a man could never accept a woman like her, no matter how hard he tried to pretend otherwise. Eventually the truth would come out. It always did.

Josie hadn't wanted to believe that Cruz was like the other men who had been in her life—controlling, manipulating, transient. But he had just given her solid irrefutable evidence that he was.

And he had broken her heart.

Chapter Ten

"Josie, what on earth is wrong with you?"

Hands on hips, Sally loomed in front of the desk, then wagged her finger in Josie's face. "That's three times in as many weeks that you've messed up the schedule. Now I've got baby aerobics and senior-citizen polka in the gym and both groups are madder than hell."

Josie rubbed her aching head. "I'll take care of it."

Sally snorted. "Sure. Before or after we both get fired?"

"I'm sorry." Sighing, Josie stood. "I guess I've been a bit out of sorts lately."

"That's the understatement of the decade." Sally's tone softened. "Look, I'll put the old folks in the auditorium so everything'll be fine, but you've got to pull out of your funk."

"I know."

Plopping on the edge of Josie's desk, Sally leaned forward. "Why don't you just call him?"

Vehemently Josie shook her head. "No, it's over."

"Doesn't look like that to me."

"Well, it is." Josie folded her arms. "Neither Cruz or Billy has been to a Scout meeting in weeks. Tran said they took a sudden vacation, then Mr. Wellington called to say Cruz had resigned as co-leader."

"Really?" Sally frowned. "Did he give any reason?"

"Something about work commitments taking too much time." Just thinking about that conversation made Josie's heart sink again. It couldn't have been more obvious that work commitments had little impact on the decision. Cruz simply hadn't wanted to see Josie. And that hurt.

Sally gave a low whistle. "So you haven't talked to him since the motorcycle race?"

"There's not much to talk about. Cruz made it pretty clear that he intended to take charge of my life. I can't live with that."

"The whole scene sounded pretty weird, all right." Sally scratched at the marred desktop. "Did you ever find out what set him off?"

"What's to find out? He just couldn't keep up the phony act, that's all."

"What phony act?"

Josie flicked her hand impatiently. "You know, a sensitive caring guy and world's greatest dad."

"Ummm. You think that was some kind of performance?"

Closing her eyes, Josie shook her head. "No, not really. But it doesn't matter."

"Of course it matters. A person doesn't twist totally out of character without pretty strong motivation. Good grief, Josie, you've got a psychology degree. You know that."

Dropping back into her chair, Josie laid her head back against the padded leather. "You're probably right, but it would have happened sooner or later. Nothing is forever."

"Right," Sally said in disgust. "Particularly when you're going to make certain of that."

Josie opened one eye. "Me?"

"Yes, you. It's called a self-fulfilling prophecy. You've spent your entire life convinced that men and women are merely passing ships in the sea of life." Dramatically Sally clasped both hands in front of her chest and sighed. "The problem is that when you find a man who really cares for you, you use everything short of dynamite to blow him away."

"That's not true," Josie replied curtly.

"Of course it's true, except you've never been in love with any of them before, so it didn't really matter to you. Now it does."

Josie felt the sting of tears and it irritated her. She didn't want to recognize the emotions swelling up inside. She didn't want to believe Sally, but she did. Everything her friend was saying was gospel truth and Josie knew it.

Had she been running toward freedom, or away from commitment?

The answer was clear.

In spite of mental protestations to the contrary, Josie had approached relationships much as had her mother. Both had been unwilling to risk pain by opening themselves, and both had been repeatedly abandoned. If Josie hadn't been searching for fulfillment from others, as had Lena, she realized that her own fear of commitment had been just as selfish.

Thinking back to the day of the motocross, Josie remembered Cruz's glazed terrified expression. Something had happened to him, something horrible, but Josie had been too indignant to question him. She'd simply assumed the worst and done what she'd always done—run away.

But then, so had Cruz.

The once-lush azalea now looked like a dead twig. Cruz blinked numbly at the shiny foliage, clipped and scattered beneath the pitiful stump. The pruning shears in his hand offered mute evidence of responsibility for the dastardly deed.

Cruz dropped the shears in disgust. Even the garden that had given him so much pleasure couldn't bring peace to his troubled mind.

He'd tried to sort through the odd jumble of his emotions, with little success. The memories that assaulted him at the race track were still haunting him.

For weeks Cruz had been plagued by nightmares, horrible dreams in which he was repeatedly forced to watch his brother's death race.

In the dream Cruz would try to run, try to save Ray, but his legs would be leaden and every movement would be agonizingly slow. The hideous nightmare would end with Cruz awaking in a cold sweat, having pulled the bloodied driver from the wreckage.

But the driver had been Josie.

"Cruzito?"

Startled, Cruz turned to see his mother standing in the garden.

Isabel smiled hesitantly. "I hope you do not mind the intrusion. Billy said you would be out here."

"No, of course not." Stiffly Cruz walked over and kissed her cheek. "I'm glad to see you."

"Are you, *mi hijo*?" Isabel's eyes were filled with concern. "Then why have you been avoiding me?"

Cruz looked away. "I haven't been avoiding you, Mother. I've simply been busy."

"Ah." Isabel perched gracefully on a lounge chair and considered Cruz thoughtfully. "We have always been honest with each other. Why do you find it now necessary to deceive me?"

Cruz couldn't answer, couldn't admit aloud why he'd been unable to face his parents these past weeks.

How could he tell them what he now knew? Their hearts had been broken once with Ray's death. It would devastate them to discover what Cruz remembered about the tragedy of that night—the tragedy Cruz had caused.

Guilt overwhelmed him, along with the horrible realization that if not for him Ray would still be alive.

Isabel saw her son's distress. "Is it the beautiful young woman who has brought this sadness to your eyes, or is it the memory of that which you wish to forget?"

Cruz felt the blood drain from his face. "What do you mean?"

"You have recalled the past. I can see it in your eyes."

Stunned, Cruz could only croak, "You . . . know?"

"I do not know all, but I know you were with Ramon that night. When the policeman brought you home, you did not even recognize us, your own parents. The doctor said it was shock, that you would soon return as yourself. But you never truly did, and the memory of what you had seen that night disappeared."

Isabel's words hit like a body blow. Cruz opened his mouth, but could utter no sound. He shook his head in disbelief then finally managed a hoarse whisper. "All these years, you knew that I caused Ray's death?"

Isabel gasped and her hand flew to her throat. "You caused nothing! How can you say such a thing? You were a child, just a child. You lived through a horror so great that your mind rejected the memory. That is all."

"No, that's not all." With both hands Cruz grabbed his head as though it were about to explode. "Ray didn't want to race that night, but I begged him to. I wanted everyone to see that my big brother was the fastest and the best. I *killed* him."

"*Madre de Dios!* No!" With surprising strength Isabel stood and grabbed her son's shoulders. "Ramon made the decision. Ramon chose his own destiny but you have allowed him to choose yours also."

"Mine?" Cruz was thoroughly bewildered. Isabel was speaking with great urgency but her words made no sense. "Ray is gone."

"No. He still exists—here." She touched Cruz's heart. "You have lived your life for him. All these years, your eyes have been joyless, filled with silent grief. Then you met Josie. She brought love to your life and laughter to your eyes. The son I thought forever lost had returned to me, to us all." Tears glistened in her dark eyes and her voice trembled. "Every day I have thanked God for sending Josie McGee. Do not lose her, my son. Do not lose yourself again."

"We're too different," Cruz whispered. "She lives on the edge, taking foolish risks. I can't deal with that."

"Perhaps it is the fear of losing her that you cannot deal with," Isabel said slowly. "You have lost your brother and your wife, suffered great pain. If you had never known Ramon and Catherine you would have been spared much grief, but you would also have been deprived of much joy. Giving one's heart takes courage, but in the end, is love not worth the risk?"

Cruz recognized the wisdom of his mother's words. He'd always held a part of him aside, safely protected from the trauma of caring too much. Josie had muscled her way into his heart and that had frightened him. He was—yes, he could admit it—in love with her.

That was the problem. Cruz simply couldn't bear the thought of losing Josie, as he had lost others he loved. Perhaps he'd subconsciously felt himself a jinx. Perhaps it had simply been safer to suppress feelings than to acknowledge them. Admittedly a cowardly ploy, repressing emotion had always been effective in the past. But with Josie nothing worked. Thoughts of her surrounded Cruz, haunting his nights, blurring his days.

Still, it had been Josie who'd walked away, although Cruz couldn't blame her.

"It's too late," Cruz mumbled. "I've hurt Josie and humiliated her in front of her friends. She'll never forgive me."

"To love is to forgive." Tilting her head, Isabel looked into her son's eyes. "To love is also to accept."

"Accept what? A woman who challenges death and laughs in the face of those who care?" Cruz whirled away, jamming his hands into his pockets. "She'll never change."

"Perhaps not. But if Josie did change, who would she then be?"

Warily Cruz glanced over his shoulder. "What do you mean?"

"What is it you love about her, Cruz?"

He shrugged. "I don't know—her playfulness and humor, maybe. I admire her courage and determination, the way she fights for what she believes."

Lifting one pale eyebrow, Isabel mused, "And if she would change those things?"

"Those qualities are an intimate part of her. Without them she wouldn't be Josie." Cruz suddenly saw where Isabel was guiding the conversation.

If Cruz had succeeded in changing Josie she wouldn't be the woman he loved.

Standing, Isabel smoothed her sleek linen skirt. "Do not fear the past, *hijo*. Remember, then let go." With that, she hugged Cruz fiercely, wiped her moist eyes and walked out of the yard.

Cruz didn't move. Surrounded by the greenery that had been his solace, Isabel's words pounded rhythmically through his mind. *Spared grief, deprived joy. Do not lose her...do not lose yourself. Remember the past, then let go.*

Thinking back, Cruz recalled moments with Josie, moments when he'd felt alive for the first time in years. In his mind he saw Josie flushed with laughter at the carnival. He remembered how she cared for other people, how she'd fretted about the boys, determined that they experience the joy of childhood.

Cruz felt humble. Yes, he'd faced tragedy in his life but he had also been blessed. As a child he'd had a stable home and parents who'd loved him. Josie hadn't. She'd been lonely and neglected, yet even in the face of such adversity Josie had never become hardened or embittered. She'd escaped the limits of her past, made something of herself. Josie had turned her own life into a crusade for helping others.

Cruz had judged and criticized, espousing the credo of responsibility while steadfastly denying his own history. It had been a cowardly escape, but the running was over.

Picking up a shovel, Cruz walked to the bare corner of the yard and began to dig Catherine's reflecting pool. Once the past had been laid to rest, Cruz could turn to the future—and to Josie.

The small frame house was as still as a tomb. Everywhere Josie looked she saw remembered images of Cruz. She pictured him squirming on the lumpy sofa, watching her with hungry eyes. The living room carpet reminded Josie of how they'd rolled in a tangled heap the night that laughter had turned to smoldering passion. Cruz's mouth had been so warm then, his arms so strong. She'd felt cherished and safe.

Now it was over.

Josie had never felt so empty, so bereft. Even as a scared sixteen-year-old facing the world alone Josie hadn't been this frightened. The thought of never seeing Cruz again, of never again knowing the thrill of his touch, his kiss—

With a gasp, Josie whirled and dashed to the bedroom. This was the one room that held no memories of Cruz, and that, Josie bitterly regretted. She'd avoided that ultimate intimacy fearing her heart would be lost forever. That fear, and all the other self-imposed terrors, had come true.

Josie was in love, urgently and desperately in love. The emotion was uncontrollable, an agonizing pressure in her soul growing stronger each day until Josie feared she would simply burst apart, exploding like an overinflated balloon.

Oh, God. She couldn't bear it.

With trembling hands Josie picked up the telephone and dialed. Even as she heard distant ringing she wondered what had made her place the call. It was as though she'd lost conscious control, propelled on pure instinct, pure need.

The ringing stopped. A garbled voice filtered through the line. Josie swallowed. "Hello . . . Mother?"

There was a moment's silence. "Jo-Jo? Baby, is that you?" Lena's disbelief turned to concern. "What's wrong?"

"Nothing's wrong." Josie felt contrite. It had been weeks since she'd called her mother. "I just wanted to talk to you, that's all."

A dry laugh filtered over the line. "The last time you called me Mother, you were four years old and spiking a fever high enough to burn bacon. What's going on?"

Before Josie could reply she heard a male voice in the background and realized that Lena was not alone. Her heart sank. "I'll call another time—"

"No, just hold on a minute," Lena pleaded, then the sound became muffled, as though the receiver had been covered by a hand.

Lena was speaking to someone, but Josie couldn't understand the gist of the conversation. She could, however, understand her mother's irritated tone. Then Lena spoke clearly into the telephone. "Just a friend," she explained. "Now, tell your mama what's got you so fried."

"Nothing—" Josie bit her lower lip and took a deep breath. "I . . . I just needed to talk to you."

Josie could almost hear Lena nodding. "It's a man, isn't it? Lord knows, I ought to recognize the symptoms. What's his name?"

No sense denying it, Josie thought. "His name's Cruz."

"Ummm, funny name. Is he nice?"

"Yes, he's very nice."

"Good. Nice ones are hard to find. So what's the problem?"

"We're different."

That seemed to tickle Lena. "I certainly hope so. That's what makes men so doggone much fun." Suddenly Lena's voice turned serious. "Why, you're in love with him, aren't you?"

"I feel . . . awful."

"That's love, all right. I should know. I was in love once."

"Only once?" Josie winced. "I didn't mean that the way it sounded."

Lena's tone was pensive. "I know what I am, Jo-Jo, and I know what folks say about me. Fact is, the only man I ever loved was your daddy. All the others—I don't know. Maybe I was looking for something I lost a long time ago. Maybe I just wanted to feel like a woman again." Lena's voice broke. "Real love isn't something you can find just because you're looking. Once it's gone you'll spend your whole life wishing after it, living in the past."

Josie heard Lena cough, then there was a soft catching sound, like a sob. It tore Josie's heart. So that's why her mother had never married—she had lost the only man she'd ever loved.

For the next hour Josie and Lena talked, sharing secrets and feelings as they'd never done before. Oh, Lena hadn't really changed, but Josie had. For the first time, Josie saw her mother as a person, both caring and flawed. She recognized Lena's loneliness, her quest for self-worth.

Perhaps all the years of men and drink were Lena's self-imposed punishment for having lost the man she loved; perhaps it was simply a quest to recapture the past. Josie didn't know but it no longer mattered. Lena was simply Lena and that was okay. Josie loved her.

When Josie finally returned the receiver to its cradle she vowed never to make her mother's mistake. Josie would not give up the man she loved; at least, not without one hell of a fight.

The following weekend Josie nervously paced, gathering the courage to put her plans into action. She'd nearly called Cruz a dozen times in the past few days but had finally decided it would be too easy for him to hang up on her. No, she'd simply appear on his front porch. Cruz Erickson was much too well-bred to slam the door in her face—she hoped.

With a deep breath she glanced over her shoulder. "Wish me luck, Walter," she mumbled, then strode determinedly out the door.

Before she got to the driveway she heard a familiar rumbling. Then there was a sputter and a cough, like a jerking engine being prodded back to life. She smiled sadly, recognizing the sound of a motorcycle. That was something Josie would miss, but it was a small sacrifice compared to a future with Cruz.

The lurching bellow grew louder.

As Josie turned the key in the door of the old sedan she'd just purchased she glanced curiously toward the street. What she saw made her jaw drop.

A huge black-and-white chrome motorcycle was bucking down the road, wickedly weaving as the harassed driver attempted to simultaneously steer and accelerate. Obviously this person was in dire need of lessons.

Josie held her breath, watching in shocked disbelief as the bike swerved toward the curb, then parked in front of her house. The helmeted rider shuddered, as though relieved to have survived the ordeal, then flipped off the ignition.

There was something frighteningly familiar about those broad shoulders. Reaching up, the man unhooked the chin strap, flipped up the visor and lifted the helmet.

Josie nearly fainted. "C-Cruz?"

Cruz grinned. "It's a beauty, isn't it? The salesman said it's got enough horsepower to climb a light pole, but I think he was exaggerating." Swinging his leg over the bike, Cruz unzipped his new bomber jacket and strode toward Josie. He ignored the fact that Josie's chin was dangling like a door on a broken hinge. "The concept of squeezing handlebars to stop and go is a bit odd but I'm getting the hang of it. Grab your machine and let's lay rubber."

"Pardon me?"

"I said let's boogie, let's skim the stripe, let's—"

Josie made a time-out gesture with her hands. "Have you completely lost your mind?"

"Not at all." Cruz looked extremely pleased with himself. "In fact my mind has never been sharper."

Frustrated, Josie stared at him, then exploded like a small volcano. "Are you trying to kill yourself? You don't know how to ride that thing—what in hell is the matter with you, anyway? Don't you know how dangerous that little stunt was? If you don't want to think about yourself, at least give some consideration to Billy. My God, Cruz, do you want your son to be an orphan?"

Cruz blinked, then his mouth twitched. Josie's cheeks heated. Talk about role reversal. Finally Josie mumbled, "I thought you *hated* motorcycles."

He didn't deny it. "I do. But you love them and I—" Abruptly he stopped and cleared his throat. Cruz stared at the ground, transferred the silver helmet from one hand to the other, then looked up and met Josie's stunned gaze. "I want to share the things that please you. I love you, Josie McGee."

"You do?"

He nodded.

"Oh." The word slipped out like a breath and Josie touched her throat.

Shifting awkwardly, Cruz looked worried. "Just 'oh'?"

Josie smiled. "Oh, *my*," she added demurely, then laughed at Cruz's dejected expression. She laid her hand on Cruz's cheek, shivering as he turned to kiss her palm.

"You've made me so happy, because I love you, too. In fact I was just on my way over to tell you so and to throw myself on your mercy."

That got his attention. His eyebrows shot up. "You were? Ummm, I'm sorry to have interrupted that. It could have been interesting."

"Not nearly as interesting as all...this." Words failed and Josie gestured limply toward the sparkling machine parked at the curb. "Cruz, you didn't have to do this. The motorcycles, the racing, none of that matters—"

Placing a fingertip gently against her lips, Cruz silenced her protest. "It *does* matter, honey." His expression sobered. "These weeks without you have been pure hell, but it's given me a chance to do some serious thinking. There's a lot you don't know about me and a lot I didn't even know about myself."

Then Josie listened as Cruz bared his heart, telling her of his brother's death and the remembered horror. When he'd finished tears slid down Josie's cheeks like hot rivers.

Josie remembered how distraught Cruz had been at the motocross, how horrified he'd been when Billy had wanted to race a go-cart. At the time she hadn't understood his terror, but suddenly everything clicked into place.

"My God," she whispered. "If only I'd known..."

"Shhh." Tenderly Cruz brushed her wet face. "It's all right. It's in the past now, and that's where we're going to leave it, okay?"

Sniffing, Josie managed a nod. "I think we've both been prisoners of our past."

"Yes, but that's over. A wise woman told me to remember the past, then let go. We have the future, and I want us to share that future together. Marry me, Josie. Say that you love me and you want to be my wife."

Wife. Marriage.

Josie closed her eyes and waited for the familiar panic. It never came. Then she realized that everything in her life had simply been leading to Cruz and to this moment. Call it fate or destiny, kismet or karma, Josie knew without doubt that their love had been inevitable.

"Yes, I love you, and I want to be your wife." Josie's voice trembled as she stroked his strong jaw.

"Oh." Cruz looked shocked, as though afraid to believe it could be true.

"Just 'oh'?" Josie chided gently.

He smiled then lowered his mouth to hers. "Oh, *my*," he whispered, then took her lips in a long sweet kiss.

Josie clung to him, savoring the moment and the joy bursting from her heart. So much happiness was frightening, but she was through running. Cruz was her future. He was her life, and whatever the coming years brought, she would never leave him.

And deep inside she felt a contentment, a comfort, a knowledge that he would never leave her.

Shaking, Cruz reluctantly released her. With a deep ragged breath he said, "Now that that's out of the way grab your wheels and let's take a spin. As you've so politely pointed out I could use a few lessons."

Josie froze. "I can't."

"Why not? It's a beautiful day and the birds are singing—"

"I don't have it."

Cruz frowned. "Don't have what?"

Rubbing her forehead, Josie sighed. He wasn't making this easy. She patted the faded compact car, hoping he'd get the message without have to verbalize the heresy.

He stared blankly. "Is that your car?"

"Yes."

"Well, that's fine, but . . ." Cruz's eyes widened. "Oh, no."

Miserably Josie nodded.

"You sold your motorcycle?"

"I, uh, thought you'd be pleased."

"You did that for me? Oh, honey, I never meant for you to..." Choked by emotion, Cruz blinked his reddening eyes and looked away. When he spoke again, his voice was ragged. "We'll get it back."

"No. That part of my life is over, Cruz. Maybe I've just outgrown it."

Attempting a scowl that didn't quite come off, Cruz insisted, "I don't believe that."

"Believe it. Besides, I think there's another way to settle our disagreement.

"What did you have in mind?"

Shrugging with a nonchalance she didn't feel, Josie said, "I don't know—maybe a game of one-on-one?"

"Ah." Cruz grinned smugly. "Get the basketball, but I warn you, I've been practicing."

Shyly Jose peeked up through thick lashes. "I wasn't referring to basketball."

Cruz looked perplexed, then his eyes rounded. "You weren't?"

"Huh-uh."

A slow sexy grin split his face. He tossed the helmet over his shoulder then scooped Josie into his arms. "And if we end up with a tie game?"

Wrapping her arms around his neck, she nibbled his earlobe and whispered, "There's always overtime."

"I want years of overtime," Cruz warned softly. "I want forever."

"Forever isn't long enough," Josie murmured. "But it's a pretty good start."

* * * * *

PASSPORT TO ROMANCE SWEEPSTAKES RULES

1. **HOW TO ENTER:** To enter, you must be the age of majority and complete the official entry form, or print your name, address, telephone number and age on a plain piece of paper and mail to: Passport to Romance, P.O. Box 9056, Buffalo, NY 14269-9056. No mechanically reproduced entries accepted.
2. All entries must be received by the CONTEST CLOSING DATE, DECEMBER 31, 1990 TO BE ELIGIBLE.
3. **THE PRIZES:** There will be ten (10) Grand Prizes awarded, each consisting of a choice of a trip for two people from the following list:
   i) London, England (approximate retail value $5,050 U.S.)
   ii) England, Wales and Scotland (approximate retail value $6,400 U.S.)
   iii) Carribean Cruise (approximate retail value $7,300 U.S.)
   iv) Hawaii (approximate retail value $9,550 U.S.)
   v) Greek Island Cruise in the Mediterranean (approximate retail value $12,250 U.S.)
   vi) France (approximate retail value $7,300 U.S.)
4. Any winner may choose to receive any trip or a cash alternative prize of $5,000.00 U.S. in lieu of the trip.
5. **GENERAL RULES:** Odds of winning depend on number of entries received.
6. A random draw will be made by Nielsen Promotion Services, an independent judging organization, on January 29, 1991, in Buffalo, NY, at 11:30 a.m. from all eligible entries received on or before the Contest Closing Date.
7. Any Canadian entrants who are selected must correctly answer a time-limited, mathematical skill-testing question in order to win.
8. Full contest rules may be obtained by sending a stamped, self-addressed envelope to: "Passport to Romance Rules Request", P.O. Box 9998, Saint John, New Brunswick, Canada E2L 4N4.
9. Quebec residents may submit any litigation respecting the conduct and awarding of a prize in this contest to the Régie des loteries et courses du Québec.
10. Payment of taxes other than air and hotel taxes is the sole responsibility of the winner.
11. Void where prohibited by law.

COUPON BOOKLET OFFER TERMS

To receive your Free travel-savings coupon booklets, complete the mail-in Offer Certificate on the preceeding page, including the necessary number of proofs-of-purchase, and mail to: Passport to Romance, P.O. Box 9057, Buffalo, NY 14269-9057. The coupon booklets include savings on travel-related products such as car rentals, hotels, cruises, flowers and restaurants. Some restrictions apply. The offer is available in the United States and Canada. Requests must be postmarked by January 25, 1991. Only proofs-of-purchase from specially marked "Passport to Romance" Harlequin® or Silhouette® books will be accepted. The offer certificate must accompany your request and may not be reproduced in any manner. Offer void where prohibited or restricted by law. LIMIT FOUR COUPON BOOKLETS PER NAME, FAMILY, GROUP, ORGANIZATION OR ADDRESS. Please allow up to 8 weeks after receipt of order for shipment. Enter quickly as quantities are limited. Unfulfilled mail-in offer requests will receive free Harlequin® or Silhouette® books (not previously available in retail stores), in quantities equal to the number of proofs-of-purchase required for Levels One to Four, as applicable.

PR-SWPS

OFFICIAL SWEEPSTAKES ENTRY FORM

Complete and return this Entry Form immediately—the more Entry Forms you submit, the better your chances of winning!

- Entry Forms must be received by **December 31, 1990**
- A random draw will take place on **January 29, 1991**
- Trip must be taken by **December 31, 1991**

3-SR-1-SW

YES, I want to win a PASSPORT TO ROMANCE vacation for two! I understand the prize includes round-trip air fare, accommodation and a daily spending allowance.

Name______________________________

Address______________________________

City____________ State__________ Zip____________

Telephone Number____________ Age______

Return entries to: **PASSPORT TO ROMANCE**, P.O. Box 9056, Buffalo, NY 14269-9056

COUPON BOOKLET/OFFER CERTIFICATE

Item	LEVEL ONE Booklet 1	LEVEL TWO Booklet 1 & 2	LEVEL THREE Booklet 1, 2 & 3	LEVEL FOUR Booklet 1, 2, 3 & 4
Booklet 1 = $100+	$100+	$100+	$100+	$100+
Booklet 2 = $200+		$200+	$200+	$200+
Booklet 3 = $300+			$300+	$300+
Booklet 4 = $400+	____	____	____	$400+
Approximate Total Value of Savings	$100+	$300+	$600+	$1,000+
# of Proofs of Purchase Required	4	6	12	18
Check One	____	____	____	____

Name______________________________

Address______________________________

City____________ State__________ Zip____________

Return Offer Certificates to: **PASSPORT TO ROMANCE**, P.O. Box 9057, Buffalo, NY 14269-9057

Requests must be postmarked by **January 25, 1991**

ONE PROOF OF PURCHASE

3-SR-1

To collect your free coupon booklet you must include the necessary number of proofs-of-purchase with a properly completed Offer Certificate

See previous page for details